ETERNAL FOREST

The Seacastle Mysteries

Book 2

PJ Skinner

ISBN 978-1-913224-45-5

Parkin Press
INDEPENDENT PUBLISHER

Cover design by Mariah Sinclair

Glass Fishing Float photo by Jonathan Zander

Discover other titles by PJ Skinner

The Seacastle Mysteries

Deadly Return (Book 1)

Fatal Tribute (Book 3)

Mortal Mission: A Murder mystery on Mars

Written as Pip Skinner

The Green Family Saga (written as Kate Foley)

Rebel Green (Book 1)

Africa Green (Book 2)

Fighting Green (Book 3)

The Sam Harris Adventure Series

Fool's Gold (Book 1)

Hitler's Finger (Book 2)

The Star of Simbako (Book 3)

The Pink Elephants (Book 4)

The Bonita Protocol (Book 5)

Digging Deeper (Book 6)

Concrete Jungle (Book 7)

Also available as box sets

Go to the PJ Skinner website for more info and to purchase paperbacks directly from the author:
https://www.pjskinner.com

Dedicated to my sister Blossy

Chapter 1

A chorus of herring gulls screaming blue murder from the roofs of Seacastle heralded the new day as I crawled out of bed, swearing under my breath. It wasn't as if I had a choice. I had to make more money or my shop would go out of business. I gazed out of the window onto the bramble patch in the back garden. At night, its impenetrable darkness projected a sinister air as if evil lurked within. Even during the day, the thought of clearing it, or tidying its thorny tendrils, intimidated me. I made myself a promise to sort it out, or to bribe my sort-of stepson, Mouse, to do so. Neither of us were keen gardeners, so it seemed unlikely to happen unless the size of the bribe made it impossible for him to refuse.

A smell of seaweed and ozone penetrated my room and reminded me that Harry Fletcher and I were due to clear out a fisherman's cottage on the bluffs above town. Hopefully, it would contain unique items to add to my stock at Second Home, my vintage shop. The old sea dog who had inhabited the cottage had moved to join his daughter in the Midlands, leaving behind his collection of marine ephemera. She had no space in her house for his things, so she gave him the choice of dying alone, or leaving his trinkets behind and integrating with her household. He chose the latter and had deserted most of his varied and peculiar collection of souvenirs of a life at sea. I couldn't wait to have a rummage through them to find interesting goods to sell.

I grabbed a towel and stood under the hot shower, pretending I didn't need two more hours of sleep. In the bedroom next door, Mouse snored, oblivious to the cacophony emitting from the gulls; probably dreaming of hacking into the Pentagon or stealing a fast car, knowing him. He's the son of my ex-husband, Detective Inspector George Carter, but that's not his fault. I threw on my clothes, and a bit of slap, and stumbled downstairs, almost treading on my cat, Hades, who hissed and ran for the shelter of his Lloyd Loom laundry basket. I had rescued him in it from the house next door, where I also met my business partner Harry, an ex-army cockney with a house clearance business. Hades had a grudge against me from the day we met, but despite that, he hadn't left my house after I brought him here. He loved Mouse and Harry, so I tolerated him back and he became a fixture at my house.

When George dumped me for his now live-in girlfriend, I not only acquired his abandoned son from his first marriage, but also found myself living in this small terraced house, known as the Grotty Hovel, with no fixed income. Meeting Harry Fletcher on my first day moving in here was a stroke of luck. He arrived to carry out a clearance on the house next door to mine and I noticed him taking out some pieces of furniture I could sell at my shop. I asked him if he would sell them to me and we struck up a conversation. We soon realised working together could be profitable, as I have a vast and general knowledge of vintage items and he has muscles and a van. He also possesses a kind heart and an iron will, both of which are qualities I find attractive in a business partner. Having Mouse and Harry in my life counted as extremely lucky, and even George has shown signs of wanting a truce, so things could be worse.

I forced myself to boil an egg and ate it with hot buttered toast, the breakfast of champions, according to my long-dead father. I raised my teaspoon to him with the last morsel of egg and then gulped down a cup of tea. Then I scrolled through the feed on Twitter on my mobile phone, a habit I had picked up from Mouse. Before Mouse invaded my life, I had lived happily as a Luddite with a bog-standard Nokia and a broken laptop. But he had installed the internet in my home and workplace and forced me to get a smartphone on a contract.

After initial resistance, I couldn't imagine how I had survived without either. I loved my phone, or at least spending time on it catching up with my journalist friends on Twitter. I lived vicariously through their requests for tips and information for their latest investigations. When I had a bout of serious depression which lost me my husband and my career, I had given up that world, but I still hung around on the fringes, gazing in the windows and fogging them with the breath of longing. Would I go back? No. I'm enjoying my life again, despite my dodgy financial situation. But I might dip my toe in if the need arose. It's like riding a bike. You might be rusty, but you soon get going if you have to.

A blast on the horn of Harry's van alerted me to his less than patient presence outside. I wrapped a colourful scarf around my neck and threw on a warm jacket. It might have been spring outside, but the weather in Seacastle was not predictable, and it's nearly always windy. I took my mobile phone off the charger and dropped it into my handbag before slipping out of the door, being careful not to let Hades out onto the road. I'm not sure if he understands the danger represented by cars, but I don't want to find out. Since the incident involving the Conrad murders, I've had a cat-flap built into the back door. It has a computer chip reader in it and only opens in response to a chip on Hades' collar. Hades used it without issue if I left the house, but if I stayed at home, he yowled loudly beside the door until I let him out. I'd change his name to Contrary if Hades didn't suit him better.

Harry leaned over and opened the door of his van, his bald pate shiny in the sun. He kept his head shaved, like a good soldier, and his sadness hidden under a cheerful, no nonsense demeanour which didn't fool me one bit. He had lost his beloved wife to cancer and there were still days he couldn't pretend to have recovered from her passing.

'Things going well?' he said. 'How's my cat?'

'All is good. Except for the cat. He's evil.'

Harry laughed.

'That's my boy,' he said, and turned up the sound.

We had matching tastes in music, being of a similar age, and soon we were both singing along to Heartbreaker by Free. That's the nice thing about our friendship. We aren't embarrassed to be ourselves and get on like a house on fire. I hope one day we'll move up a level, but for now we are like teenage friends on an adventure and that's fun too.

The sea dog's cottage sat in a row of weather-beaten cottages that lined the road out of town along the coast which straggled along until it reached the scruffy carpark for the Shanty pub, our favourite watering hole. It occupied the end of the row behind a wall of grey flint set in concrete. One of the side walls sloped inwards and had caused the roof to bow and some slates to slide into the gutter. Large streaks of seagull excrement discoloured the whitewash and added to the air of neglect.

'From the look of it, the previous owner got out just in time,' said Harry.

'It could be lovely, given some TLC,' I said.

'Fantastic view.'

I turned to look out to sea, and the wind caught my scarf, tugging it from my neck and sending it into the air like a streamer. I grabbed at it, but it flew away like a knight's pennant. Luckily, it wrapped itself around a lamppost, and Harry pulled it down and wrapped it around my neck. I grinned at him and pecked his cheek.

'Last one in's a sissy,' I said, and sprinted towards the front door.

Harry grunted and ran after me, but he couldn't stop me from reaching the door in front of him and turning the key. The door swung open and the musty air made me wrinkle my nose in disgust, but once my eyes adjusted to the light, I forgot about the smell. A dozen glass fisherman's floats hung from the ceiling in heavy rope nets. They caught the sunlight as they twisted in the breeze entering the cottage, sending rays of coloured light piercing the darkness. Various species of fish, the results of taxidermy, sat on shelves in their glass cases in undersea tableaux. Their state of repair suggested a vintage, possibly Victorian origin, and I wondered if they were responsible for the odour.

'Pike, carp, trout, perch, rudd and roach,' said Harry, pointing at the cases.

Then he peered at one label.

'This is right up my alley,' he said, and puffed out his chest. 'Did you know that J Cooper and Sons were the pre-eminent taxidermists of fish since the late Victorian Era?'

'Seriously? You know about this stuff?'

'I had an uncle who paid them to mount a pike in the 1950s.'

I guffawed.

'That sounds like some sort of weird fetish.'

'Only to your dirty mind. Do you realise that these are quite valuable?'

'How much is quite?'

'I'm not sure. At least a monkey, possibly more,'

'Five hundred quid? I'll take them all.'

Harry rubbed his chin and shook his head.

'Okay, but I want the pike. For my house.'

'The pike? Are you going to mount it?'

'Hilarious. Get the blankets.'

We packed all the glass floats and the fish into the van along with the captain's chair, a quaint cupboard with wonky shelves and cubbyholes, and a wooden mermaid, crudely carved and painted on the prow of a ship. Harry wanted the mermaid too, but I vetoed that.

'You got the pike. I want the mermaid.'

'Are you going to mount that in the shop?'

I grinned at him.

'You're such an idiot.'

'Let's get this lot over to the shop so we can make loads of dosh,' said Harry. 'I'll come back for the rest.'

I rolled my eyes at him.

'They'll be queueing outside the door for the fish specials,' I said.

While my clients lacked any interest in fish beyond the chippy, I had a shrewd idea who might buy them. Grace Wong, the owner of the expensive antique shop at the posh end of the high street, would fall over herself to sell them in her shop. I just needed someone to look up their value on the internet first and I knew the man for the job.

Chapter 2

Both the glass cases of the mounted fish and the fisherman's floats were cushioned by blankets in the back of the van, but Harry drove with exaggerated care to Second Home, the tension in his shoulders visible as he negotiated the potholes on the road from the fisherman's cottage. My vintage shop is situated down at the cheap end of the high street near the Co-op, inserted between a charity shop and a dodgy mobile phone outlet. There used to be an Italian café across the road, but the proprietors moved back to Napoli, and it radiates abandon with its Formica tables and chrome chairs in a sad pile in the window. I would quite like to buy them, but I'm not sure how to contact the owners.

The lack of a decent coffee shop on our end of the high street led me to open one of my own, The Vintage, which occupies the front room of the first floor of my building. I own the whole thing, bought with an inheritance from my parents for almost nothing when Seacastle was even less fashionable than it is now. It has three stories; the ground floor which has the main sales area and small kitchenette and stockroom, the first floor with the café at the front and the office at the back, and the second floor which is used for storage now but has potential to be used as a small flat. I know Mouse has been eyeing it, but I quite like him staying with me at the Grotty Hovel, so I'm waiting for a showdown.

The main sales area on the ground floor is an eclectic mix of 19th and 20th century furniture and fittings. I planned to hang the glass floats in between the lamps and chandeliers which dangled from the ceiling. I wasn't sure if I could bear to sell them, but maybe I'd just take one or two home and force myself to get rid of the rest. Someone like me who combines hoarding tendencies with a love of antiques faces a constant struggle to run a vintage shop. It's a pitched battle between love and money, and love wins rather often in my case. At least my house now looks like me and is full to the brim with vintage goodies, instead of the beige minimalism I had to tolerate when married to George.

Harry staggered in with the largest of the mounted fish, a rather splendid trout, which looked as if greed might have been his undoing. I asked him to put it front and centre in the main window of the shop, where Grace or Max Wong would be sure to spot it on their way past. The label on the case read 'IRT Trout 5 lbs. Caught by Mr P Rowe at Wimborne, 21 July 1938'. I wondered if it had been bought at auction, or perhaps a clearance before they became fashionable. We distributed the cases around the shop, including a couple in the café upstairs. They made quite an impression with their varnished scales and glassy eyes. I couldn't decide if I liked them or not, but I had a feeling they would soon be snapped up by eager punters. Harry had to go back to the cottage to empty it of the remaining furniture and artifacts, but before he left, he hung some of the glass floats up amongst the lamps on the ceiling, using their rope netting. They gave the shop a nautical air which I rather liked.

'Get selling,' he said, as he left, giving me a big wink.

I found it hard not to fancy him and to stick to our agreement, but it became progressively hard to keep. I didn't have any time to contemplate my relationship with Harry as the doorbell jangled and Ghita, all of a twitter, burst into the shop. Ghita Chowdhury is one of my closest friends, the owner of a soft heart and a (over) sensitive character. She is also incapable of keeping a secret. Her eyes glistened with excitement as she pecked me on the cheek and then rushed to the kitchenette to put on the kettle. Tea being an essential ingredient for her in any sharing of gossip. While the kettle boiled, I watched her shifting from foot to foot on her tiptoes with some amusement. Ghita had huge brown eyes and long, luxuriant black hair, and she struggled to hit five feet in height, something which galled her greatly. I did not interrupt her ritual by making a sarky comment about her stature, as I knew her well enough not to spoil the moment for her.

Instead, I looked around at the mixture of antique and eclectic goods that formed the basis of my wares. I had concentrated on collecting vintage, rather than antique goods, which gave me more leeway and less pricey stock. My favourite items for now were the glass fisherman's floats and the wooden mermaid, which reminded me of Roz Murray. New stock always made me excited. At that moment, the doorbell jangled as Roz blew in like a mermaid on acid. For once, her tousled locks were a natural dirty blonde colour instead of some outlandish mixture of neon. Her cheeks were flushed pink from cycling along the Seacastle promenade from Pirate's Harbour where her husband Ed kept their boat. They often slept aboard, lulled to sleep by the changing tides. Their house, although cosy, did not have the lure of the harbour with its ozone and seaweed infused air.

'What's new?' said Roz and seemed about to launch into her usual stream of consciousness.

People called Roz 'the Foghorn' for a reason, laying claim to the title of Seacastle's biggest gossip. I put my finger to my lips and lifted my chin to alert her to Ghita's Zen like mood. I could see she had news of her own, but Ghita rarely claimed the limelight, so Roz could wait. Roz sighed in frustration. I held firm.

'Come upstairs to the café and I'll make us a latte,' I said.

'Is there any milk in the fridge?'

'If not, you can nip out and get some.'

Enough milk remained to make two small lattes. Ghita came upstairs with her cup of tea as I poured the hot milk into the coffee shots. I patted the padded bench beside me and Ghita plumped herself down on the velvet cushions. She took a sip of her tea and licked her lips in anticipation.

'You know the council is debating the feasibility of setting aside an area on the seabed for a kelp forest?' she said.

'I've heard about this marine protection area,' I said.

'My husband's a fisherman,' said Roz. 'I'm sick of hearing about it.'

Ghita ignored her.

'Well, my manager, Marion Pocock, put me on the committee supervising the progress of the MPA negotiations, reporting directly to her.'

'That Kraken promoted you? Well done. That's some feat,' I said.

'Didn't she tell you that you were too stupid to live once?' said Roz, who could never resist baiting her.

Ghita frowned and put her hands on her hips.

'Honestly. Can't you let me tell you my news without interrupting?'

'Sorry. Go ahead,' said Roz, with bad grace.

'Anyway, as I was saying, I got promoted to the committee and there's this man, David de Frontenac. Well, he's a dreamboat. He looks like the male lead from a Regency romance novel, with black curls and azure eyes, and the body of a knight errant.'

'How poetic. It seems as if Prince Charming has ridden in on his charger,' I said. 'That's not normal council business.'

'Shut up, Tanya. He's so gorgeous. He really is just like a dark Prince Charming. I think I'm in love.'

'Love or lust?' said Roz.

I elbowed her, and she shut up.

'Have you talked to him?' I said, trying to be practical.

'Um, not much. He's awfully busy, you know. He's an eco-warrior.'

'Back to the charger,' said Roz. 'Does he wear armour?'

'Metaphorical armour,' said Ghita. 'He's fighting for nature and the planet.'

'He sounds lovely,' I said. 'Will we get to meet him?'

'I don't think so. He's terribly busy. But he's talked to me several times, and he doesn't have to.'

'He's not blind then,' said Roz. 'You are gorgeous.'

Ghita blushed.

'Thank you. I know I'm not.'

'If he hadn't noticed you, he would need a trip to Specsavers,' I said.

'There's plenty of time to make him yours,' said Roz. 'He'll be here for a while. The battle has only just begun.'

I could tell she didn't mean Ghita's fight for recognition. A look of alarm clouded Ghita's face.

'You won't make this difficult for me, will you?' she said.

'It's our living,' said Roz. 'Do you expect me to lie down and let them trample all over hundreds of years of tradition?'

'No, but you need to hear the arguments first. I think it's a great idea.'

Roz sighed.

'Try telling Ed that. He's determined to fight to the death on this one.'

'Do all the fishermen feel the same?' said Ghita.

'I think there are a couple of waverers, but the others are holding firm.'

'I hope there's some science behind this and not just wishful thinking,' I said.

'The people leading the campaign say so,' said Ghita. 'And David Attenborough mentioned their project in an interview once.'

'David Attenborough?' said Roz. 'We're doomed.'

She faux-fainted onto the velvet banquet and lay there with her eyes closed and her hair in a halo around her head, looking like a Pre-Raphaelite painting. Ghita sighed.

'No wonder it's difficult to make any headway, when people just make silly jokes and stick to what they know.'

'You'll make all the difference in your new role,' I said. 'This calls for a celebration. Does anyone fancy a piece of cake?'

Ghita shook her head.

'I can't stay,' she said. 'They increased my hours at the council, so I won't be able to cover the shop as often. I hope that doesn't make it difficult for you.'

'No, I'll think of something. I'm sure Mouse will jump at the chance to earn more money.'

Ghita gulped down her tea and gave us both a wet kiss before dashing downstairs and out onto the street, her hair streaming behind her.

'She's fallen hard,' I said. 'He sounds out of her league to be honest. Remember what happened the last time she thought someone fancied her?'

Ghita was thoroughly lovely and kind and clever, but she could be naïve about men. I always kept an eye out for someone she could love who would love her back, but her high standards for grooming and appearance meant that her choices were often shallow or self-absorbed men who could be cruel and not the right man for her.

'Trust Ghita to fall in love with the man leading the campaign to wreck our industry,' said Roz. 'Do you think she does it on purpose?'

Despite appearances, Roz and Ghita were close friends, but I heard a tinge of bitterness in her voice.

'Is everything all right?' I said.

She shrugged.

'I've been fighting with Ed a lot recently. The stress of leading the resistance to the MPA has made him grumpy. And we're desperately short of money.'

The Ed I knew personified grumpy. He had a reputation for being tough on his crewmates and always seemed to fire and re-hire them. Roz brought out the best in him, so if his bad moods were affecting her, things had definitely deteriorated.

'She doesn't do it on purpose, you know. Ghita is in love with love. It will blow over.'

'But she seems oblivious to the damage that the project will do to our living.'

'You seem to be sure of its effects, but have you done any research? Maybe it's a good thing in the long run?'

Roz stood up and stuffed her hair into a tangled bun and huffed.

'Trust you to take her side. She's not as defenceless as you think.'

'I'm not taking her side. I'm trying to play devil's advocate here. There may be an upside to this project.'

Roz sniffed.

'I haven't seen one yet.'

'Give the council a chance to get the negotiations going. You never know, they may turn it down, and all of this will have been a bad dream.'

'A nightmare, you mean.'

'With a gorgeous leading man?'

A grin crept onto her face.

'I can't wait to see this vision. Ghita is besotted.'

'There, you see. Things are looking up already.'

Chapter 3

When Ghita fell for the glamorous eco warrior, I assumed she had her usual school girl crush on an unobtainable celebrity. I'm not faulting her taste, but he sounded way out of our league, and I imagined her passion would fade eventually, like the fad for spinners and skinny jeans. Mind you, I had expected men to get bored with beards too. How wrong can you be? Her new-found role at the council took up most of her time, so I found myself confined to the shop more than I would like. Mouse could run the café easily enough, but he knew next to nothing about my stock and I hadn't got time to price everything individually. The taxidermy fish haunted the place, swimming amongst the furniture, but so far nobody had shown any interest. Mouse wanted to put them on eBay, but I couldn't face yet another app I didn't understand.

I had installed myself behind the display cabinet that doubled as our front desk to do the accounts, when a face I recognised from the past popped around the door. Lexi Burlington-Smythe pushed her way into the shop and stood beaming at me from the doorway. I jumped off my stool and gave her a fond hug.

'Surprise!' said Lexi. 'I bet you never thought you'd see me again.'

This counted as the understatement of the year. The last time I had seen Lexi Burlington-Smyth ('pronounced like Hive, darling'), she cadged a lift home to Wiltshire in a friend's Jaguar. She waved to me from the back seat, her mascara flaking and her face blowsy with drink, and I had never seen her since. We had met a few times before that night at glitzy media events in London, but on that memorable evening we had both worn the same dress by coincidence. Probably because of the amount of champagne she had imbibed, Lexi had let down her hair more than normal, and thought it would be amusing to pretend to be twins. Always one for a laugh, I agreed. This ruse went down a storm with the men at the party, many of whom were taken in by it. Lexi and I were similar in stature and both had curly chestnut hair, but she had a touch of refinement no makeup could imitate. Her high cheekbones and unblemished skin suggested unheated mansions and riding out with the hounds.

'On borrowed horses. We're nouveau poor, you know.'

Unlike many of her friends, she didn't have a trust fund to dip into, and had found her niche introducing her wealthy peers to impoverished good causes. I hadn't heard from her in years, but I treasured fond memories of her, despite her buttoned up emotions and stiff upper lip.

'You haven't changed a bit,' she said.

I smiled. In one sense, it was true. I still had my chestnut curls (my crowning glory according to George) and my love of pixie boots, but life's tribulations had excavated wrinkles around my eyes like stream beds in chalk. Lexi had amazing genes, and designer jeans, and still hung onto her thirties with no sign of relinquishing them. Despite running in media circles for the best part of a decade, she hadn't felt the need for Botox or fillers, unlike the celebrities she hung out with. They now resembled the gargoyles on Salisbury Cathedral with their weird contorted faces and bloated lips. Her pale blue eyes still twinkled in her alabaster face like a china doll left in a cupboard and untouched by time.

'Neither have you,' I said. 'Did you get home okay?'

Her eyes widened with delight at my still remembering our night out.

'It depends what you mean by okay. I had a narrow escape.'

For a fleeting moment, I caught a shadow of misery in her face, but it vanished in an instant to be replaced by her no-nonsense facade.

'Me too. Have you got time to catch up? I've got a handy café upstairs.'

She gave my arm a squeeze of assent and we climbed the stairs. While I made us a couple of lattes, she nosed around and had a good look at the back office, a large room with almost no furnishings. She spent some time gazing into the glass cases at the taxidermy fish.

'Those are splendid,' she said. 'My father would love one. Are they for sale?'

'They are. They're not cheap though.'

'Oh, don't worry about that. His second wife is loaded. She pays for everything.'

'I can give you a list of species labels if you like and you can ask him which one he would prefer?'

'Excellent.'

'What brings you to Seacastle? It's not on your normal list of haunts at this time of year. Shouldn't you be skiing somewhere with clients?'

'Normally I would be, but I'm involved in an important project right now. The proposed kelp sanctuary off the coast. You may have heard of it.'

I found it hard to avoid hearing about the sanctuary with Ghita and Roz at loggerheads over it, but I just smiled.

'It has come to my attention.'

'Well, I'm running the negotiations with the council and the other stakeholders. We're hoping to come to an agreement about designating an area offshore as the sanctuary. The council seems keen, but I'm not sure about anyone else yet.'

'I'm not too clear on the benefits of it. I know the local fishermen are up in arms.'

'You should get David to explain about the kelp. He's our expert. But there's vehement local opposition to the idea, and I need to find ways of convincing people of its value.'

'Rather you than me. Is there anything I can do to help?'

'I think there is. I'd like to rent your office space. If you can provide it furnished with internet and sockets, I have a generous budget that I would prefer to spend with you than at the temporary office units in the commercial centre. The café is a bonus. We could hold meetings here instead of at the council offices. A relaxed environment might help us have frank conversations we can't get in their stuffy meeting rooms. If you agree, we could start here on Monday.'

I pretended to consider it, but I was in no position to turn her down. My Piscean enterprise had not produced the results I had hoped for. Grace had walked past my shop window half a dozen times without so much as a glance at my trout. And spending more time in the shop had only resulted in extra cake and less income. It was just as well that Ghita also ran the Fat Fighters Club in her spare time. Without those exercise classes, I might have had to go up a jean size.

'I'd be thrilled,' I said. 'I'm not sure if we can be ready by Monday, but I'll do my utmost.'

Once we had settled on a price, we fell to chatting about the old days. I told her about George and his new other half, and she told me about her close shave with the man in the Jaguar. She told me she had given up men for Lent about four years ago and forgotten to take up with them again. I almost told her about Harry, but something held me back. After all, what did we have besides a working partnership?

After she had left, I called Harry.

'I remembered you had a friend with a warehouse full of second-hand office furniture. Do you think he would rent me a few desks and chairs for a month or two?'

'What's this for?' he said.

'An old friend has asked if she can rent the office space at Second Home. I could keep the place going for months with what she's offering.'

'He owes me a favour. I'll see if I can borrow some stuff, or get a good deal for it. Leave it with me.'

Mouse's friend Goose turned up with some wall sockets the next day. Like many of Mouse's friends, he had been in various scrapes with the law, but the impending arrival of his first child had brought him down to earth with a bump. Mouse still hung around with the more-dodgy members of his crew, but as long as he didn't bring them back to my house, I refused to get involved. His father took a dim view of these lads, but like Goose, they were growing up and thinning out as life caught up with them. Goose accepted a coffee after installing the sockets at bench height along the opposing walls of the office. He smacked his lips in appreciation.

'That's wonderful coffee. I'll be back,' he said.

'I'll definitely use you again if I have any electrical installation that needs doing. How did you get started?'

'I did my NVQ level three in electrical installation at Chichester College. They gave me a grant because of my background.'

He avoided my eyes, but I knew he had been in trouble with the law when he was younger, just like Mouse.

'Afterwards, they apprenticed me to an electrician, but we didn't get on so well, so I recently branched out on my own.' He looked around the shop. 'I do CCTV installations as well, if you're interested, although I don't think you need it much.'

I laughed.

'It's not all junk you know,' I said.

He blushed.

'I didn't mean…'

'I know you didn't. How much do I owe you?'

After he had left, I looked around the now furnished office and I felt a frisson of excitement. I had not considered renting it out before. It offered me an additional source of income and a captive audience for the café, a win-win situation. Maybe I'd see more of Ghita. She'd been absent from the Second Home since the start of the project, and I missed her breathless excitement and fragrant hugs. If she could avoid winding Roz up, and vice versa, things could go back to normal.

Chapter 4

The next Monday, I rose with the lark. Not really, but it felt like it. I had forgotten to give Lexi a set of keys, so I needed to be at the shop before them to let them into their office. To tell the truth, I think I did it on purpose. The whole idea of having tenants intimidated me, but it was too late to change my mind. I glanced in at Mouse before I went downstairs and felt a swell of emotion as I watched him sleep cuddled up with Hades. They were like peas in a pod despite being boy and cat. Both were quick to anger and fond of a sulk, but their diffident outer shells held in a torrent of unresolved emotions. Maybe Lexi could find some work on the project for Mouse. If we were going to indulge in nepotism, I wanted him to benefit. He had a genuine talent for research, and to be honest, hacking. I know we're not related, but I feel like he inherited some of my investigative genes by osmosis. I suppose it's not surprising how intuitive he is, considering his father is a D.I.

After I had filled Hades' bowl with fresh water, I removed half of a mouse from beside the fridge door. Hades would be useful in the post-apocalyptic era if we needed meat, but I wasn't too keen on finding disembowelled mice on my kitchen floor. In case he still felt hungry, I spooned some fresh cat food into his bowl. Mouse loved Hades, but neither of them were over domesticated. I had shown Mouse how the washing machine worked, but he just shrugged and left his clothes on the floor in his room, a bit like Hades' offerings. I suppose I acted like that too, when he tried to show me a new app. The division of labour worked fine for now, so I didn't complain. After a couple of years practically bedridden with depression, I had emerged to find myself divorced and ignorant of new technology to a frightening extent. Mouse had rescued me, and I him.

I left my car at home as I did on sunny days and walked to work along the promenade. I carried several crusts in my pocket, planning on feeding them to the juvenile herring gull who hung around the wind shelter where I often stopped and gazed out to sea. On reaching the shelter, I sat on the bench breathing in the sea haze, and breathing out my problems. My therapist had taught me to imagine my depression as an entity. The nasty little thug had materialised as an evil green sprite who mocked and belittled me. Once I had become used to his presence, I had to put him on a boat and push him out to sea where he would float away until he disappeared over the horizon. The first time I visualised this process to its completion, it felt as if an enormous weight had been lifted and I wept copious tears. Now I did it just for the immense joy of seeing him scream and cry in protest as he disappeared from view. Childish, I know, but oh so satisfying.

After distributing the crusts to the gull and a couple of scavenging rooks, I left the shelter and turned off the promenade up King's Road to its intersection with the high street. Second Home's pretty Victorian shopfront always gave me a lift as I walked across the street and approached the front door. The painted wooden window frame had suffered a little during our stormy winter and had flaked, but the deep red colour enticed the punters to step in and look at my wares. I stuck the key in the lock and shoved the door open, pushing the junk mail to one side. It rarely contained any real post, but I always checked every envelope in case someone had left me a fortune and their lawyer was desperately trying to get hold of me.

I dumped the post on the counter and took a deep breath, which I let out with a cough. The shop smelled strongly of fresh emulsion paint, which caught in the back of my throat. I went straight upstairs to open the windows at the front and back of the floor to let the sea breeze clear the air. I stopped to admire the new back office with its relatively new desks and chairs and the sockets installed by Goose. A frisson of anticipation ran up my back at having direct access to the negotiations for the kelp forest. There were sure to be some juicy discussions and twists and turns before any agreement could be reached. My background as an investigative journalist had turned me into a nosy parker at the best of times.

I heard the doorbell jangling downstairs and Lexi's voice calling out.

'Cooee! It's us. Are you here?'

'Hi Lexi. Yes, come on up. The office is ready.'

She ran up the stairs and gave me a hug. Then she let herself into the office, making noises of approval and bagging the best desk. My first meeting with David de Frontenac did not strike me as auspicious. He came upstairs slowly with his handsome face contorted in disgust and did not greet me. Instead, he pushed past to peer into the glass cases containing the taxidermy fish.

'How could you?' he said.

I blinked.

'How could I what?' I said.

'Fish have feelings too, you know.'

'They're Victorian. I doubt they're still suffering.'

'Honestly David, give it a rest for a minute,' said Lexi, poking him in the ribs. 'This is Tanya Bowe, an old friend of mine. She's letting us the office,'

He grunted. Behind him, a slightly flustered young black woman came up the stairs two steps at a time on her long, slim legs. She stuck out her hand.

'I'm Amanda Grant,' she said. 'Lexi's P.A. and the project accountant. The office looks perfect.'

'Thank you. You can use the facilities up here for refreshments. Mouse is in charge if you want a barista type coffee.'

'Mouse?' said Amanda.

'My stepson. He should be here soon. I can make you a coffee if you're desperate, but I don't have his silky skills with a latte. By the way, Lexi, Mouse is a computer wizard, and a brilliant researcher, so please sort out a deal for a few hours' work if you need help.'

They filtered through into the office. David shot me a filthy look over his shoulder. Ghita could have him. I could see his physical attractions, but I doubted romance would be on the cards after that start. He had quite a strong physical resemblance to Mouse, but his nasty character had marked his face with an almost constant sneer. My Mouse trumped the prince every time.

I wandered back downstairs and did the accounts. I always found transferring the items from my hastily scribbled notes from the house clearance into the Excel sheet to be mind numbing, but if I left it too long, I also found it tortuous. Harry had taken fifty pounds for each of the taxidermy fish, but besides Lexi, the general reaction to them had been horror or revulsion. I hoped I hadn't made a terrible mistake. The notebook in front of me filled with doodles as I lost concentration, and soon, I had wandered into a daydream which looked a little like something from the Yellow Submarine with taxidermy fish.

The doorbell jangled, and I almost fell off my stool as Roz breezed in, her curls bright green, matching her fisherman's sea blue smock and green leggings. She resembled the wooden mermaid even more than I had remembered. I pointed it out to her, and she laughed.

'I'm flattered,' she said. 'Have you taken up carving in your spare time?'

'It looks remarkably like you. Guess who I've got upstairs?'

'I can't. Don't keep me on tenterhooks. You know how I love juicy gossip.'

'Ghita's environmentalists, including Prince Paramour.'

Her eyes opened wide.

'Seriously? What are they doing here?'

'I rented them the back office.'

She puffed out her chest.

'I'm going to give them a piece of my mind.'

'Don't be silly. I've only just moved them in, and I need the rent.'

'I promise I'll be gentle,' she said, spotting one fish in its glass case and running a finger along it. 'Great buy. I love them.'

Before I could object, she had marched up the stairs and stood in the office door with her hands on her hips. I followed her up in a panic.

'So, you're the bleeding hearts who are saving the kelp and bankrupting the fisherman,' she said.

Lexi laughed, Amanda pouted, and David, well, he appeared struck dumb. He stared at Roz until his eyeballs dried out and he was forced to blink.

'I'm not sure that's entirely fair,' said Lexi. 'I could explain how it works if you've got a minute.'

'Do you work here?' said David, recovering his voice.

'Sometimes,' said Roz, her lazy drawl a warning sign I recognised.

'And you don't object to murdering fish to use them as decoration?'

Roz choked and guffawed with laughter.

'You can give them the kiss of life if you're so worried about them,' she said. 'Fish are for eating.'

David sniffed.

'I'm a vegan. I don't eat fish or eggs.'

'But you've got leather shoes on…'

David had the good grace to blush.

'I'm mostly vegetarian, actually.'

'How do you know someone's a vegan?' said Roz, to no one in particular. 'Because they tell you.'

She laughed again, but she shoved her arm through his.

'Why don't you have a cup of tea and tell me all about it?' she said.

He appeared mesmerised and didn't resist, and she dragged him into the café. He allowed himself to be led to the couch. Lexi shook her head.

'Now that's a new one for me,' she said. 'I've never seen David bested before.'

'Roz is quite a gal,' I said. 'She'll have him wrapped around her finger in no time.'

'I hope not. He's supposed to be going out with me.'

'Roz's married. I was speaking figuratively.'

'I'm only joking. It's been over for a while.'

I noticed Amanda's sullen expression. Did she fancy him too?

'Actually, it might be good if David listens to Roz's concerns,' I said. 'Her husband is a fisherman, and he's not at all happy about the kelp sanctuary. Maybe David can explain to Roz why it's a good thing. She can introduce him to some of the strongest opponents of the project if he wants to make headway with them.'

I handed her the keys.

'By the way, these are for you. Please make sure you double lock the door when you leave.'

'I will. And I'll let you know tomorrow which of the taxidermy fish I want for my father.'

'No rush. I expect there will still be lots of choice. Would you like to come and have a drink in the Shanty sometime? It's got a superb view of Pirate's Bay.'

'Sounds like fun. Should we wear matching outfits?'

'I'm not sure Seacastle is ready for that.'

'Nor was London. But we did it anyway.'

I grinned. Maybe having tenants would be more fun than I had imagined.

Chapter 5

Later that morning, Mouse turned up to run the café during the lunchtime rush. We had office staff regulars who turned up with their sandwiches and ate them with a coffee at the window seat tables overlooking the High Street. They arrived around the same time, often with laptops and phones on the go, and Mouse knew them all by name. I didn't mind them eating their lunch there, as they could be seen from the street and it encouraged other people to come in and have a coffee. This led to more sales of vintage items because of the extra footfall. I introduced Mouse to Lexi who batted her eyelashes at him and pinched his cheek. I knew he hated it when people did that, but he didn't object, especially when Lexi offered him some paid research. Amanda blushed when introduced and, from the look on Mouse's face, he found her pretty cute too. They were both tall and slim and nerdy, so I guess it was inevitable.

Ghita arrived at the shop at lunchtime, dressed in one of her most colourful outfits. Her eyes shone with excitement as she bounced upstairs to rendezvous with Lexi about the next council meeting. Unfortunately, she bumped into Roz arm in arm with David leaving the shop to meet some of the local fishermen. Roz's husband, Ed, still objected to the sanctuary, and she intended to round him up with the rest of the fishermen for a preliminary chat. Ghita's face fell as she noticed David's rapt expression. He seemed to hang on Roz's every word. Roz, as usual, was oblivious to Ghita's reaction. Sometimes I wanted to give her a sharp kick, but I doubt it would have helped.

'Where are you going?' said Ghita.

'Roz wants to introduce me to some opponents of our plans. We'll bring them back here for a quick get together after lunch to give them an intro to the project. I thought a less formal setting might help them relax around me,' said David.

'Can I come?' said Ghita.

'I don't think that would be a good idea,' said Roz. 'They don't like strangers much.'

Ghita deflated.

'I'm sure you're right,' she said.

'You can't go anyway,' I said. 'We need you here. Lexi and I require your expertise. Let Roz take David away so we can get on with it.'

'Quite right too,' said Lexi from the staircase. 'We don't want David cluttering up the place when we have important strategies to set up. He's hopeless at that sort of thing. Aren't you, darling?'

But David had gone, following Roz out of the shop like a rat after the Pied Piper. Ghita swallowed and nodded, her disappointment palpable.

'Your outfit is fabulous,' said Lexi. 'Come up and tell me where you bought those superb pantaloons. I must know.'

'You do look rather wonderful,' I said.

'It's a pity no one else noticed,' said Ghita.

'David?' said Lexi. 'Oh, he's infatuated with Roz already. Don't worry, he'll soon get over it. He has the attention span of a goldfish, and I should know. You need someone much better than that piece of fluff to keep up with you.'

Ghita appeared mollified by this and followed Lexi upstairs. While Mouse played barista, we shut ourselves into the upstairs office and got to work. Lexi's father was a retired Colonel or General or something like that and she had inherited his capacity for planning and logistics. I had underestimated her abilities, and I listened to her explain the strategy with a growing admiration. Lexi was the most dreadful snob, but she had a kind heart. She claimed to have modelled herself on the Mitfords and used phrases from Love in a Cold Climate all the time.

'As long as you're not channelling Unity,' I said, when she had first told me.

I also noticed how she made Ghita feel like a key member of the team and forget her disappointment about David. This side of Lexi had not been obvious to me in our previous meetings, but I promised myself to pay more attention in the future. People are always surprising when you meet them in their element. I had wrongly assumed her to be just a social butterfly, but Lexi had the nous to be a four-star General. No wonder David de Frontenac had hired her, if that was how it worked. She had called him darling, and hinted at a liaison of some sort, but who knew? Lexi's emotions were MI5-level secrets. She had a brittle charm that enveloped her like an eggshell, and nobody penetrated inside.

Somehow, Lexi had located the telephone number of Frank Burgess, the owner manager of the local dredging company and she charm bombed him into joining us for David's meeting. We set up a screen for the presentation against the back wall of the café and laid out the chairs in vague semi-circles facing it. Mouse went to the Co-op and bought supplies of milk and biscuits to keep everyone going.

'Am I the only one who's nervous?' I said.

'It'll be fine,' said Lexi. 'David's not the nicest person on the planet, but he's knowledgeable and approachable, so I don't expect we'll have any major problems.'

'I wonder if anyone will fancy buying a taxidermy fish?' I said.

Lexi laughed.

'That's the spirit,' she said. 'Supposedly, people need to see something seven times before they buy it.'

'I must tell Grace that. She's walked by dozens of times and totally ignored the fish. I bought them for her, you know.'

'Someone will love them. You'll see. Oh, I sent photos of them to my father and he wants the fat trout. I'll take it with me when I visit them and bring you back a cheque.'

A cheque? What a pain. I hadn't stepped inside a bank for years, but money is money. I beamed. David and Roz returned shortly afterwards with two local fishermen, Bert Higgins, and Len Graves in tow, as well as Ed Murray, Roz's husband. Ed had just got back from fishing overnight, his normally handsome face haggard with exhaustion and his red hair stiff with salt. Roz handed me a plastic bag, which she had in the poacher's pocket of her coat. It contained a mermaid-style dress, made from blue and green cotton with organza petticoats. A woman in Seacastle specialised in this sort of ethereal wear and Roz couldn't resist them.

'Can you keep this here for me? I bought it in a sale on my way to Pirate's Bay, and I haven't told Ed yet. He hates me to spend money on clothes.'

I stuffed it behind the desk, meaning to give it to her later, when Ed was not around. She did not sit beside him for the talk, preferring to bask in the glow of David's admiration, and, by the look of the scowl on his face, Ed had noticed. Roz liked to keep Ed on his toes. Their jealous reconciliations were legendary.

Frank Burgess, the dredging guy, arrived last, and after perfunctory introductions, David launched into his tried and tested summary of the project. He introduced himself as an eco-warrior with the backing of David Attenborough, which made a few eyes roll, including Lexi's. Apparently, they shook hands once at a function and David had taken that as a personal endorsement. I couldn't tell if it impressed anyone else. At this stage, Harry turned up and wedged himself into a chair at the back, giving me a wink. I hadn't invited him, but Mouse gave him the thumbs up, which told me who had. I wasn't against Harry attending the meeting. He had a no-nonsense aura from his time in the military that dissuaded people from acting out. David pointed at his slides.

'So, why does Seacastle need a marine protection area?' he said.

'It doesn't,' muttered Frank.

David ignored him.

'The shallow seabed along the coast used to be covered in forests of kelp and other seaweeds which stretched for hundreds of miles. These acted as nurseries and protection for the eggs and hatchlings of commercial fish stocks. They also harboured mussels which attach themselves to the fronds and filter bacteria, algae, detritus, and other free-living organisms from the water keeping it clean. If you remove the kelp, you reduce the survival rate of the hatchlings and the number of fish that reaches adulthood. Also, without mussel beds, the water can become contaminated with algae causing blooms. Has anyone here noticed a reduction in fish stocks over the years?'

Len and Bert nodded. But Bert harrumphed.

'Everyone knows that's because of the French,' he said, and Ed laughed.

'He's right there,' said Len.

'The Frogs leave no fish for us,' said Bert. 'It's nothing to do with kelp as far as I can see. It will reduce the area we can trawl and our catches will fall.'

'But I thought foreign trawlers couldn't fish inshore,' I said.

'Correct,' said David. 'They need to be licensed by the British government.'

'They're still selling licenses to the French,' said Len. 'What difference will the kelp make if we can't keep the fish?'

'Kelp grows in shallow waters where there's plenty of sunlight. Large fish rarely swim in these areas. Only mussels and hatchlings.'

'The mussel boats won't like this plan either,' said Bert.

'It's been done before with significant results in Lyme Bay, but it takes time to establish itself again. Once the kelp grows to adult size, it forms the ideal environment. It's a pity we can't examine a kelp bed around here to get a baseline for the type of sea life which benefit from its presence, so you can understand this.'

'Actually, you can,' said Ed.

'That's right,' said Len. 'There's a small patch of it over the wrecks.'

'Which wrecks?' said David.

'There's an area where you can't trawl or dredge because of the carcases of WWII ships on the bottom. The kelp still grows there in abundance,' said Ed.

'Wow. That's news to me. Can we dive over the wrecks?' said David.

'Sure,' said Bert. 'They're only about thirty metres down. The shelf has a gentle slope near the coast.'

'I can take you out,' said Ed. 'I've got a friend who can supply the gear if you've got the cash.'

'That would be fantastic,' said David. 'I'd need a wreck guide though, for safety.'

'I'll lead the dive,' said Len. 'My dive master's licence is still valid.'

'You're a dive instructor?' said David.

'I had a misspent youth in Bali.'

'Girlfriend?' said David.

'Yup. I stayed for a year with her, but they wouldn't let me marry her, so I came home.'

'You mean she threw you out?' said Ed.

They all laughed.

'I need to see this for myself,' said Bert. 'I simply don't believe in this scheme.'

'And me,' said Roz.

'Anyone else?' said David.

'I can't swim,' said Ghita.

'Me neither,' said Amanda.

'And I only swim in heated pools,' said Lexi. 'You'd never catch me in there.'

'Count me in,' said Harry. 'I haven't been diving for years.'

'Me too,' I said, to my surprise.

I hadn't been diving since before I had depression, but I didn't want to miss the chance to see a real kelp forest.

'Can you arrange for tanks for all of us?' said David. 'The project will pay for the dive. We can collect all sorts of data with so many of us going. Also, you should get a good idea of the kelp's essential role as a habitat.'

'I've only been down to look at the wrecks before,' said Ed. 'I never thought to examine the kelp. I don't mind organising a dive, but I need to get some sleep first. Can we do it tomorrow?'

'Tomorrow will be fine. I hope everyone can make it. It's much easier to understand once you've seen the evidence.'

'I don't see how it helps me,' said Frank. 'The further out we dump the sediment the more it cuts into our profits.'

'Councils will just have to pay more to dredge their harbours,' said Lexi.

'I'll never support it,' said Frank, his face turning puce with irritation. 'The environment can look after itself. It's all hearsay and codswallop about the damage. We've been dredging and dumping sediment for years with no problems.'

'Just because you can't see the damage doesn't mean there isn't any,' said David.

Frank pushed back his chair, sweating with irritation.

'You've got a bleeding cheek coming down here with your hoity toity friend, Miss Stuck Up, and telling me what to do. Anyway, I've got friends in high places who'll put a stop to this.'

He headed down the stairs without giving David a chance to reply. A brief silence fell on the group.

David coughed and frowned.

'I hope you guys will give us a chance to convince you,' he said, finally. 'Change is hard, but I'm sure you'll reap the dividends in a relatively short time.'

'I'm only listening to you because my wife told me I had to,' said Ed. 'I don't mind letting you use my boat, but I'm far from giving you my vote.'

'I'll work on him,' said Roz, giving him a cheeky smile, which melted him instantly.

'Good,' said Amanda. 'Because I need David's full attention from now on.'

She folded her arms in defiance of anyone who would disagree. It occurred to me that Ghita wasn't the only one at the project with a romantic interest in David de Frontenac. That man could have started a harem.

Chapter 6

The next morning, we assembled at Pirate's Bay in the chill air of the dawn. Even the seagulls were still tucked up in their nests as we boarded the boat and put on our life jackets. The sea looked as calm as a millpond and a ribbon of fog hung over the wind farm as we chugged out of the harbour on our mission to inspect the remnants of the kelp forest. Len and Bert represented the fishermen, David, the project, and me, Roz and Harry came along to help record any life we found over the wreck. Ed had called in a favour from a friend who ran a diving school. He had borrowed digital cameras in waterproof casings and plastic clipboards with special pens for taking notes on the sea life we saw in the kelp. David had brought his own phone and specialised case with him, but we others took one of the hired ones.

After half an hour of cutting through the gentle waves and bouncing around more than was comfortable, we arrived at the dive site, which had been marked with a series of red warning buoys. A gentle swell lifted the boat, but nothing difficult for diving. David gave us all a quick lesson on how to focus the cameras and take pictures underwater. He explained what to look out for in the kelp patch by showing us pictures of juvenile fish and hatchlings. Len and Bert nodded and muttered between themselves, but they didn't dispute the facts. I couldn't wait to explore the kelp reef, but I dreaded the cold. Harry noticed my tight expression. He tucked his arm into mine and gave me a grin.

'I haven't been diving for years,' he said. 'I hope I remember what to do.'

'It's bound to be freezing. The Caribbean is more my temperature. I hope I don't get pneumonia.'

'You've got plenty of padding,' he said. 'Seals don't get cold.'

I tried to punch his arm, but he moved out of range. I ran my finger over my throat and he laughed at me. Bert came out of the cabin with an assortment of wetsuits.

'Pick one that fits and put it on. There's no point standing around and getting cold.'

I rummaged about in the pile of neoprene and came up with a medium-sized suit. Everyone seemed to get one which satisfied their requirements, and soon we were all stripping off. It felt weird undressing in front of Harry. We had never seen each other's bodies unclothed before, and I wasn't convinced that blotchy legs with massive goose pimples were a turn on. I sneaked a glance at his naked torso and admired his tattoo of a winged dagger on his left shoulder. It had an inscription on a scroll under it, but I couldn't read it from where I stood.

Luckily, the struggle to pull on the suits distracted everyone from their embarrassment, and soon we were all suited and booted in neoprene and I felt toasty and warm in my snug one. Bert pulled his hood over his head and made us giggle. He resembled a walrus with his large moustache poking out of the hole for his face. I noticed David gazing at Roz who undressed in a languid striptease. I hoped Ed had not seen it too. The boat did not have room for the full-on brawl it might have provoked.

Those who were going on the dive buddy-checked each other's tanks and respirators before jumping overboard off the platform at the back. The freezing water hit me like a brick wall and I surfaced, wheezing with pain. I cleared out my mask and persuaded myself to put my head back under water despite the sensation of pins being stuck into my ears. Harry gave me the thumbs up sign and I reciprocated. I must have looked miserable, because he reached out and took my hand and we swam downwards together, clearing our ears as we went. I had forgotten how painful it can be until you make them equalise with a pop, like landing fast asleep in an aeroplane and waking to the sharp pain in your eardrums.

Once I got accustomed to the temperature, the crystal-clear water surrounding us dazzled me. The waters on Seacastle beach always looked murky with algae and seaweed fragments mixed with mud, but here you could see the bottom clearly from twenty yards up. As we descended, we approached the long fronds of kelp which waved at us from the deep. Getting closer, we could see the clumps of mussels attached to the strange rocks poking out of the sand, and to the fronds themselves. Then I realised the things I thought were rocks, were actually pieces of rusted metal and we were swimming directly over a wreck. Shoals of tiny fish shimmered between the fronds, slipping into the shadows as we approached. I had not realised how rich the undersea environment could be in England. My first dives had been over barren sands with the odd crab scuttling along them, but I had been lucky enough to dive in the Red Sea, which teemed with life. I never expected to see something similar at Seacastle.

I swam around the clumps of fronds, mesmerised by the beauty and fruitfulness of the forest of kelp, and I did my best to take photographs of the elusive hatchlings, but I could not recognise them. I planned to examine the photographs on deck and make a list instead. David had not been exaggerating. I wondered what the fishermen made of it. Perhaps they would see the sense of voting for the project after all. I followed the line of the wreck, tracing the patches of mussels and other shellfish. No trawler could dislodge them without getting snagged in the metal struts. No wonder the area had thrived as a sanctuary for wildlife. I swam closer to take photographs of the colonies and disturbed a small octopus, which emitted a jet of water as it shot away and landed on the sand. It camouflaged itself almost immediately and I couldn't spot it any more. The jet had uncovered a starfish whose tiny legs scrabbled to rebury it.

Then I felt Harry tug at my hand and he tapped the air gauge on my regulator signalling that we needed to finish and return to the boat as my tank had almost run out. I couldn't believe the time had gone by so fast. We surfaced as a group, taking a stop halfway up by hanging onto a line for one buoy which marked the wreck. We took off our tanks while still in the water and handed them to Ed who stowed them for us. Harry gave me a hand getting back on the platform as the movement of the boat made it difficult. When we got back onto the boat, Len went into the cabin to talk to Ed, and Harry and I sat on a bench wrapped in towels, discussing the things we had seen. The sound of a furious row escaped from the cabin and flooded the deck in swear words. I hoped Len and Ed didn't come to blows. I could feel Harry tensing beside me, always ready for action. Then, out of the corner of my eye, I saw David try to kiss Roz. She avoided his effort, but she did not move away. He reached out a hand to stroke her face. Before I could react, Ed stormed out of the cabin and shoved David hard in the chest.

'Keep your filthy hands off my wife,' he said. 'And you, come into the cabin where I can keep my eye on you.'

Roz bit her lip, but she didn't reply, and followed him meekly inside. Ed ejected Len and slammed the door shut. Then he swung the boat around to head back to Seacastle. David did not seem the least put out by Ed's furious reaction to his flirting with Roz. Instead, he shrugged and scrolled through the photographs on his phone. The sounds of giggling soon replaced the initial yelling match from the cabin as Ed and Roz's rapprochement took its usual course. David sat with Len and Bert, answering their questions about the project and looking at the photographs on their cameras. I borrowed his phone so I could admire his photograph of some hatchlings hiding amongst the kelp. It reminded me of the movie *Finding Nemo*.

As we headed for the harbour, I leaned against Harry and enjoyed an excuse for closeness. We had an agreement to take things slowly, but now and then I liked to test the boundaries, both mine and his, to see how we were progressing. Since the Conrad case, I had the extra complication of George's change in attitude to me. It made me less sure we had put our relationship to bed for good, and more confused about my feelings for Harry.

When we got to shore, David collected all the cameras and told me he would take them to the shop.

'Amanda has some photo software on her computer. She can download the images from today and make a list of the species we observed. We can add a collage of the species to the presentation we are making tomorrow. When people see what we found in one small patch of kelp, they may understand how it would help to create the sanctuary.'

'Mouse can help make a list of our findings over the wrecks. He's great at that sort of thing.'

I cadged a lift home with Harry so I could have a hot shower at my house and return my core temperature to normal. Bert set off for a pint at the Shanty. David promised to join him later. He claimed to have an appointment, but I imagined he had had his fill of the grumpy fishermen for the day. Roz and Ed were still bickering and giggling, but that was par for the course, so we left them to it. I didn't expect to hear any more about it.

Chapter 7

The first summit meeting at the council turned out to be rather a damp squib. All the principal stakeholders turned up and were handed a copy of the latest presentation. Ghita had done a fantastic job on an agenda which dealt with all the major talking points, and silence reigned as people devoured the contents of the report. The time for the meeting to start came and went, but nobody from the project team had turned up. I called Lexi to find out why they were delayed, but she did not pick up. When people shifted in their seats and looked at their watches, Ghita asked me if I would start the presentation. Her pleading overcame my initial reluctance, and I used the notes under the slides to begin the talk.

Once I began to speak, I relaxed as I remembered far more of the presentation than I had imagined. David had enthused all of us with his lucid descriptions of the kelp forest and its myriad of benefits for sea life. Despite the niggles, the dive on the wreck site had crystallised my support for the project. My enthusiasm must have been obvious, as when I looked out at the stakeholders, I could see their rapt attention. Any new idea will meet resistance, but I felt like this one had palpable benefits for even the most jaundiced attendee. I almost forgot about the absence of David and Lexi until I realised Roz and Ed were also missing. It seemed rather strange after their determination to make sure the fishermen got a fair deal. They could also contribute to the discussion after their visit to the kelp patch.

When none of them had appeared by the end of the presentation, Ghita's boss, Marion Pocock, adjourned the meeting.

'After all the trouble I've been to, you'd think they'd bother to turn up. Typical over-privileged, posh people. They've no more interest in the environment than I have.'

She folded her arms and made a thin line with her lips. I got the impression we wouldn't be getting her vote no matter how good the project was. But where were Lexi and David? I couldn't understand it. Something serious must have stopped both of them from turning up. I galvanised myself and suggested that we meet again in a week at the same time and place. To tell the truth, I didn't feel up to answering questions about the project and felt relieved to be going back to the shop. Frank Burgess objected strongly to the adjournment.

'I've got questions,' he said. 'You can't ride roughshod over hundreds of years of history, just because some ponce from London tells you to grow an underwater garden.'

'We understand you have concerns, Mr Burgess, but there is no need to be objectionable,' said Ghita.

Marion Pocock smirked.

'I've put the wheels in motion,' said Burgess. 'You don't know the truth about that eco idiot. He won't be bothering us again. Why do you think he didn't turn up today?'

'I'm sure there's a reasonable explanation,' said Ghita. 'They're serious people.'

'And who do you think you are? Some jumped-up junior from council ranks who thinks they can tell us about running our businesses. It's a disgrace.'

Several other people murmured in dissent at his attitude, but they were already filing out of the meeting room. Marion Pocock did not back Ghita up. Ghita's flushed face told me of her distress, and I squeezed her waist discreetly. She gave me a tiny smile.

'Don't just stand there. Get the room cleared out. We need it for the budget meeting later this morning,' said Pocock.

I picked up some water glasses, but Ghita shook her head.

'I'll do it. Why don't you get back to the shop and find out what's going on?'

'There had better be an explanation for this,' said Pocock. 'It's a shocking way to behave. I'm all for progress, but bad manners are not fashionable at any age.'

'You have every right to be annoyed,' I said. 'I have no idea why they didn't turn up. I promise to find out and let you know.'

'It's a bit late now,' said Pocock. 'Little Lord Fauntleroy will have to do a lot better than that if he wants my vote.'

She swept out of the room on her high horse. Ghita rolled her eyes.

'That's all I need,' she said. 'Marion is not at all convinced by the sanctuary. She thinks it's all green party nonsense. I had almost persuaded her to keep an open mind until this debacle.'

'It's only a minor setback,' I said. 'I promise to keep you posted. Are you working all day today?'

'No, I'll be over at the shop this afternoon, if I can bear to watch Roz canoodling with David.'

'I'll have a word with Roz about it. I know she likes to make Ed jealous, but she's gone too far this time.'

'See you later, then.'

I drove to the shop expecting to find some drama in progress, but only Mouse and Amanda greeted me as I came in.

'Where are the others?' I said.

'I thought they were with you at the council meeting,' said Mouse.

'Do you mean they never arrived at the office?'

'I haven't seen any of them.'

'How strange. Lexi isn't answering her phone either. I guess we'll have to wait until they turn up,' said Amanda.

While Mouse went upstairs to get the café ready for the lunchtime rush, I took a bottle of vinegar and some old newspapers and polished the glass cases of the taxidermy fish. They had years of fly faeces and other dirt adhering to them and that made it hard to appreciate the beauty of the fish inside. Mouse laughed when he saw me scrubbing away at the dirt.

'You made a mistake with those fish,' he said. 'Harry got the best end of that bargain buy.'

'I offered him a cut of the profits, but he wouldn't take it.'

'Clever man.'

I ignored him and carried on polishing. Shortly afterwards, the shop bell jangled and Roz came in, looking bedraggled. I stopped cleaning the glass when I noticed her haggard face.

'Roz? What on earth's the matter?'

Her face crumpled, and she fell into my arms, weeping. Roz never cried. She often shouted, and roared with laughter and sang out of tune, but she hadn't ever shed a tear, as long as I had known her. I made her sit down and waited for her sobs to subside.

'What on earth's the matter?' I said, when her shoulders stopped heaving. 'Has something happened to Ed?'

She looked up and seemed to be about to speak when she spotted someone coming.

'Don't tell him I'm here. Please,' she said, before running upstairs and heading for the attic flat. I ran after her, but she slammed the door in my face. Flummoxed, I gave up and shrugged my shoulders at Mouse. Before either of us could comment, the bell rang out again. D.I. George Carter, my ex-husband and Mouse's father, stood at the counter. He did not make a habit of visiting me. In fact, I struggled to remember the last time he had come to the shop.

'To what do we owe this pleasure?' I said, intending to make some frivolous comment, but then I saw his expression.

'I'm afraid I've got terrible news,' he said. 'We've had to arrest Ed Murray. The lads have taken him down to the station for processing.'

'But whatever for?' I said.

'Ed's in prison?' said Mouse.

George nodded.

'It's pretty bad I'm afraid.'

'You'd better come upstairs and have a cup of coffee,' I said, and hung the closed sign on the door.

George followed me upstairs and had an awkward handshake with Mouse. He had thrown his son Andrew, known as Mouse, out of his house a few months previously and I had taken him in. They had since reconciled and the truce had held, but only due to them not seeing much of each other. Mouse offered George a coffee, which he accepted. I waited for him to explain about Ed's arrest.

'We received a tip off,' said George, sipping his drink. 'Or at least the coastguard did, about Ed Murray's fishing boat. They took one of the coastal patrol vessels out to sea and boarded it there. They carried out a thorough search and found a certain David de Frontenac's body hidden behind the bulkhead. I understood from Mr Murray that Mr de Frontenac had the use of the back office on this premises.'

I noticed his slip into police jargon as he dealt with official business, but nothing could stop my yelp of surprise.

'David dead? Are you sure it's him? He was fine last night.'

George nodded.

'We're pretty sure. Ed identified him right there. He must have intended to dump the body at sea, but the coastguard got there before he could carry out his plan.'

'But why would Ed murder David? That makes little sense,' said Mouse.

My face flushed as I remembered Roz hiding upstairs in the loft. Had she gone too far this time? Ed would do anything for her. But murder? That seemed far-fetched even for a hothead like Ed Murray.

'Who called in the tip-off?' I said, hoping to distract from my burning face.

'Anonymous, I'm afraid,' said George. 'From an old-fashioned phone box.'

'Is there still one here that works?' I said.

'Yes, it's on the road east out of Seacastle near the Blue Lagoon chippie.'

'I'm surprised call boxes still exist,' said Mouse. 'Those things are stone age.'

'It tells us something about the person who called in the tip off,' I said. 'Nobody Mouse's age knows how to work them.'

'I hadn't thought of that,' said George, and he patted my knee. 'You've still got it, haven't you?'

He gave me a sly smile, which made my heart leap despite myself. For an instant, I recalled how it felt to be in love with him.

'Tanya's a sleuth,' said Mouse. 'She should run a detective agency.'

George rolled his eyes and took his hand off my knee.

'As if I needed that sort of interference in my work. You are forbidden to set up an agency or to interfere with this case.'

'I have no intention of interfering,' I said. 'But Ed is my friend. You can't expect me to stand by without helping.'

'That is exactly what I expect.'

'Can you just tell me one thing? Was the caller's voice male or female?'

'It's none of your business. And if you see Ed's wife, tell her we need to speak to her as a matter of urgency.'

Mouse couldn't help glancing at the doorway to the attic, but I distracted George by jumping up.

'If there's anything I can do, you will let me know, right? But meantime, Mouse and I are up to our necks in work here.'

George looked around at the empty shop, disbelief written large on his face.

'It looks like it,' he said. 'Well, I certainly have a lot on, so I'll be going. Can you ask that woman who runs the project to get in touch with me down at the station? She has also disappeared.'

'Lexi? Yes, of course. As soon as she turns up, I'll bring her there. Do you want her mobile number?'

'Text it to me, please. I've got to go. The forensic team is down at Pirate's Bay with Ed's fishing boat. I need to see how they are doing.'

'What should I tell Roz?'

'Tell her to come and see me at the station. Also, she should bring a bag of clothes and toiletries for Ed. He won't be going anywhere for a while.'

Chapter 8

After George had left, I let myself into the loft door and crept up the stairs. I hadn't been there for months and I had forgotten how filthy the attic rooms were. A single bulb swung from a wire in the passageway. I wondered if Roz had been eavesdropping on our conversation.

'Roz? Come out. I need to talk to you right now.'

Loud creaks came from the room at the back and I edged forward to look inside. There weren't many places to hide in the attic, so I soon found Roz huddled under the eaves. She emerged when I beckoned her, with a sheepish look on her face.

'What the hell is going on?' I said. 'George just informed me they have arrested Ed for murder.'

'Murder? That's ridiculous. He can't have. Why would he kill Len?'

'Len. Is he dead too?'

'What do you mean too? Who else is dead?'

The look of bewilderment on her face appeared genuine and probably reflected mine.

'Come downstairs,' I said. 'We need to talk.'

She followed me down to the café and accepted a coffee from Mouse without comment. Usually, she would have said something about the quality of the coffee or the server, but Ed's arrest had left her dumbstruck.

'I don't understand,' she said, pushing her wild mop of hair off her face. 'Who is dead, and why have they arrested Ed?'

'The coastguard boarded Ed's boat out at sea and found a body behind the bulkhead. They think he planned to dump it out there.'

'A body? But that's impossible.'

'What do you mean impossible? Isn't there enough room for a body there?'

'No, there's plenty of space, it's just…'

'Just what? You aren't making any sense.'

'How did Len die?'

'Len's not dead, as far as I know.'

'Well, who then? I don't get it.'

'David.'

Roz jumped to her feet, throwing coffee everywhere, her face drained of blood.

'David? No. But he wouldn't, not my Ed. I don't believe it. I was only trying to make him jealous. He couldn't have.'

She stumbled to the stairs.

'Where are you going?' I said.

'Ed needs me. I have to tell the police. It's all my fault.'

'Tell them what?'

But she ignored the question and ran down the stairs almost bumping into Lexi, who leapt out of her path. Roz burst through the door out onto the street and ran towards the police station.

'What on earth's got into Roz?' she said. 'She looks as if she's seen a ghost.'

'You mean you haven't heard either?' said Mouse.

'Heard what? I've been home to visit my parents. Daddy had a nasty turn. My stepmother called me last night, and I went straight there. I took the taxidermy trout with me; I hope that was okay. My father loved it, oh, and I've got a cheque for you somewhere.'

She rummaged in her bag. I exchanged glances with Mouse. He stood up and headed downstairs. I put my hand on Lexi's arm. She glanced up and waved a cheque in the air.

'Here it is. I knew I had it somewhere.'

'Please listen to me for a moment. There's been an accident on Ed's boat.'

To my disappointment, she put the cheque back into her handbag.

'Is Ed okay?' she said.

'Sort of. The police have arrested him.'

'Is that why Roz… What happened?'

'It's David. He's been murdered and the police think Ed did it.'

Lexi's jaw dropped and she shook her head.

'David's dead? Oh my God.'

She went as pale as snow and grabbed the arm of the chair.

'I'm afraid so. I'm sorry.'

'But how. When? Are you sure?'

'George came to tell us.'

'Your ex? Isn't that weird?'

'Not really. He knows Roz works in the shop sometimes.'

'Oh, I see. But why would Ed kill David? I don't understand. Didn't Ed change his mind about the project?'

'I'm pretty sure his motive wouldn't be the project.'

'You mean Roz? But David had crushes on people all the time. Nobody took them seriously.'

'Ed didn't know David well. Not as well as you, anyway.'

Lexi's eyes filled with tears. She took a handkerchief out of her handbag and blew her nose into it.

'We were close, despite everything. It seems so unlikely. How could David be gone? Are you sure they haven't made a mistake?'

'As sure as I can be right now. George asked me if you would go down to the station when you turned up. I expect he wants information about David's next of kin.'

'Next of kin? Oh, I don't think I can.'

'Why not?'

'It's complicated.'

'He's dead. George will soon find out if he had any secrets. He'll be looking for a motive, and that means searching David's past and present with a fine-tooth comb.'

Lexi sighed.

'I can identify the body.'

'Are you related?'

'No, but David is, was, an orphan. He didn't have any siblings that I know of either.'

'Nobody to mourn him?' said Mouse. 'That's sad.'

'What would you like to do about the project? Should we put it on hold for now? Marion Pocock was livid when you didn't show up this morning.'

'It wouldn't be fair to David. The project is his legacy now. I'm going to do everything I can to force it through. But I can't do this alone. You must help me.'

'Of course, if that's what you want.'

Lexi stood up and straightened her jacket, the model of efficiency again. Any feelings she experienced buried deep under the tweed casing. I wondered if she had a heart at all.

'I'm off to the station,' she said. 'Will you come with me for moral support?'

We left Mouse in charge of the shop and set out. Seacastle high street cheers up considerably at its eastern end. The charity shops give way to chain stores and coffee franchises which blend into high-end bistros and expensive shops selling French soap and overpriced antiques. As we neared the station, Lexi's demeanour became strained, and she dawdled more. Despite the importance of our mission, Lexi stopped in front of Max and Grace's shop to admire their superior items. I didn't tell her some of the best had come from my shop and now had much higher prices. I didn't blame her for procrastinating. It seemed so odd for David to be stored in the police morgue. He should have been lying on a bier with flowers like a storybook prince, not on a marble slab.

Sally Wright looked up from her keyboard at the reception desk in the police station and raised an eyebrow.

'I know Roz Murray is entitled to conjugal visits,' she said. 'But aren't you a bit late for yours?'

I ignored her. Sally, despite her butter-wouldn't-melt appearance and blonde Shirley Temple curls, specialised in winding people up. She usually called me Mrs Carter, even though she had replaced George's live-in-lover Sharon Walsh, at the desk and knew we had been divorced.

'This is Lexi Burlington-Smythe. She worked with the victim. George, D.I. Carter asked to speak with her,' I said.

'Ah, okay, I'll buzz him. Wait here.'

We waited in the lobby surrounded by message boards covered in leaflets with instructions on reporting a crime and getting help for trauma after being the victim of an assault. The wave of petty crime had ensured reactive policing had long since replaced proactive policing in Seacastle. I could remember when mothers were still the first line of defence against crime, but that made me feel like a fossil. The swinging doors bulged open and George pushed his way into the lobby. He spotted us sitting on the plastic chairs and bustled over.

'You must be Alexandra Burlington Smythe,' he said.

Lexi's face fell. No one ever used her full name.

'Am I under arrest?' she said.

'Of course not. It's just an informal chat.'

'Then I'd like Tanya to be with me, if that's okay.'

George rolled his eyes and emitted an exasperated sigh.

'Follow me,' he said.

He led us to a small interview room with glass walls. Curious glances were followed by awkward smiles and half waves from George's colleagues. They had all dropped me from their social circles since the divorce, but it was no great loss. I gave them brusque nods of acknowledgement as befitted the discarded spouse of their D.I. George steepled his fingers and took a deep breath.

'First, I understand you were close to the deceased. Please let me express my deepest condolences for your loss.'

Lexi sniffed and dabbed her eyes with a spotless linen handkerchief.

'We knew each other most of our lives.'

'And you worked together for how long?'

'About ten years.'

'Did you have a relationship with him?'

Lexi feigned shock.

'Pardon?'

'I apologise, but we need to establish the facts of the case. Were you going out with him?'

Lexi smirked.

'Now and then, David got bored with philandering and made a pass at me.' She pursed her lips. 'And sometimes I let him.'

'So, he used to play the field?'

'No female felt safe with David around. He loved variety; any age, any race, any religion. He wasn't fussy.'

'Did he have any enemies?'

'Dozens. Just follow the trail of broken hearts and jealous husbands.'

'Did David know Roz Murray?'

Lexi glanced at me and bit her lip.

'They were acquainted. He had a crush on her, I think. Roz is an attractive woman.'

'Did they work together?'

'Not exactly. Roz acted as an unofficial liaison officer with the fishermen.'

'I understand your project would have affected their livelihoods.'

'Oh yes. It would have improved them immeasurably, but not straight away.'

'I heard it would restrict their fishing grounds. They can't have been pleased about that.'

'The benefits of the project are long term. We need to persuade opponents of the project it would be worth it.'

'And did Ed Murray object?'

'Initially, but David took them on a dive over the wrecks to see the kelp patch. He told Amanda he had a good chance of getting Ed on side.'

'And when was that?'

'When he left the memory cards with photographs of the kelp forest with her, after the dive.'

'And where was this?'

'At Tanya's office.'

'And what did Ed think of David's crush on Roz?'

'I don't know. You'd have to ask him.'

George rubbed his chin. A gesture I recognised.

'And how did you feel about it?'

Lexi sighed.

'Bored.'

'Why?'

'Because his crushes inevitably disrupted his concentration and caused drama.'

'But not emotional distress?'

'Not to me, officer.'

George turned to me.

'And what about you?'

'What do you mean?' I said.

'Did you fall under his spell? Roz said he was abnormally handsome, like a fairy-tale prince.'

'David was handsome, but I prefer the more rugged, well-worn sort of bloke,' I said, looking him straight in the eye. 'As you know.'

He grinned, but he hadn't finished with me yet.

'I understand you went on the dive with them. Did you notice any tension or arguments on board?'

I felt his eyes bore into me. I couldn't lie under that sort of scrutiny.

'There were several flashpoints. I heard Ed arguing with Len in the cabin.'

'And David?'

'He tried to stroke Roz's cheek at one stage and Ed told him not to touch his wife again.'

'Or what?'

'He didn't say. He shut himself in the cabin with Roz afterwards and I heard more shouting.'

'Shouting? What were they saying?'

'I don't know, but it turned into giggling. They row constantly. Ed is super jealous, you know.'

George nodded. I felt stupid. I hadn't meant to say that. He's not a D.I. for nothing.

'Can I see Ed?' I said.

'Not now. He hasn't been charged yet.'

'Will he be out on bail?' said Lexi.

'It depends on the judge. It's not looking good so far.'

I understood his pessimism. Ed had at least two powerful motives. George would still have to prove means and opportunity though. He stood up.

'That's all for now, ladies. You know your way out, Tan.'

Outside the station, Lexi slipped her arm through mine.

'I can see why you married him. That man is a hunk. Do you think Ed murdered David out of jealousy? Or was it because of the sanctuary?'

I dropped her arm.

'Ed didn't murder anyone. I know him.'

But did I? It wasn't as if we were close friends, and Roz always called him a hothead. Could he have lost his temper with David and then panicked? Lexi took my arm again.

'I think we should let the police get on with it. Do you fancy a quick reccy in Grace's shop?'

Chapter 9

The next day, Ghita turned up at the shop wearing black. Her puffy eyes told me all I needed to know about her reaction to David's demise, but she didn't want to discuss it. Usually, she would have unburdened herself over a cup of tea, but she greeted me coldly and went upstairs to help Lexi plan the next stakeholder meeting at the council. Something about her mute reaction to David's death made me nervous. I judged it safer to let her come to me, as I sensed her bristle when I tried to approach her.

Mouse turned up asking for Amanda.

'She's upstairs,' I said. 'What are you two up to today?'

'We had planned to download the photographs from the dive cameras. I'm not sure whether we should go ahead.'

'The ones David brought to the office after the dive?'

He shrugged.

'I don't know. I suppose so.'

Amanda came downstairs to join us.

'This is very important,' I said. 'How did you get the memory cards? Did David give them to you?'

She couldn't look me in the eye.

'He left them on my desk,' she said. 'I had to leave early.'

'You didn't see him?'

'No. I told you. I found them on my desk yesterday when I came to work. He had a copy of the keys for the shop, you know.'

I didn't. But she appeared to be lying. Lexi had told George that Amanda had been in the office when David dropped the cards in, and that David had told Amanda he thought Ed would vote for the sanctuary.

'Do you have a copy of the keys too?'

'Yes, we all do.'

Amanda went back upstairs to the office with Mouse to download the photographs of the dive from the camera cards. They sat snuggled up close, and I suspected they were becoming better acquainted by the day. I had never seen Mouse show an interest in a girl his own age before. He acted tough and hung around with some dubious pals, but he often chose the company of my women friends. Once he had even attended one of Ghita's Fat Fighters' classes, causing consternation and hilarity in equal measure.

The classes were an institution in Seacastle. Long-term members like me had long since given up pretending to be serious about losing weight. It was more like a jolly social club where we immediately recharged any calories we'd used with coffee and cake. Ghita did a good job keeping the classes fresh and interesting, so we always had numbers. Other people came and went, but the core membership of me, Roz, Grace, Joy, who ran the Shanty pub, and sometimes Flo, the pathologist, stayed constant. After the class, the ladies insisted he came along to the traditional debrief. He had not come to another class, despite Ghita's pleadings, but maybe Amanda would enjoy it. I planned to ask her at the right moment.

Neither Amanda nor Lexi seemed to mourn for David, which struck me as odd. I guessed his womanising ways had taken the shine off for both of them. Lexi soon had Ghita hard at work designing a leaflet extolling the virtues of the sanctuary. I wondered if I could ask her for the payment for the taxidermy fish without causing offence. She had claimed to be carrying the cheque in her handbag, and the money came from her 'loaded' stepmother, so I didn't see the harm in reminding her. I took in a breath to shout up at Mouse to make us all a coffee, when Roz came into the shop, uncharacteristically subdued. She had black bags under her eyes and her hair sat in a wild bun on her head, like an eagle's nest on top of an electricity pylon. Her dress hung loose around her waist; its belt loops empty. I had never seen her like this. A wave of pity swept through me.

'We're about to have coffee,' I said. 'Come upstairs.'

I shut the shop door. We hadn't had a single customer all morning. I wondered if the fish were actively putting people off. Personally, I loved them, and coveted a small perch with a spikey dorsal fin, making it look like the piscine version of a Stegosaurus. Harry had put his pike in pride of place over the fireplace in his sitting room. What would Cathy have made of it? I couldn't imagine. I had no clear picture of his deceased wife's character.

Talking about her did not come easily to him. He had the army habit of prioritising action and quashing his feelings. My battle with depression had made me prefer action to feelings too, so we had an alliance of action that worked well for us.

Roz did not notice Ghita's obvious distress. She greeted her and gave her a hug. Ghita stiffened instead of reciprocating and kept her arms down by her side. She then sat as far from Roz in the café as she could. Lexi, Mouse and Amanda sat with her, as she stared at the back of Roz's head with something approaching hatred. Roz spooned two sugars into her coffee. She stirred it manically until I put a hand on her arm to stop her.

'Is there any news about Ed?' I said.

'Plenty of news, none of it good,' she said, grimacing.

'Have they charged him with anything?'

'Not yet. But it's only a matter of time.'

She grabbed my hand tight enough to hurt.

'You've got to help him.'

'I don't see how. George won't let me have any information, and he's confident this case is open and shut. I know it's hard to accept, but Ed may have lost his temper and killed David by mistake. Perhaps he pushed him and he fell backwards and hit his head on something hard enough to crack his skull? Why was David inside the fishing boat, anyway?'

Roz did not have time to answer. Ghita had jumped up and charged over, her face puce with indignation.

'It's all your fault,' she said. 'You killed David by the way you behaved, and Ed will be in prison for life now because of you.'

Roz's mouth fell open at this tirade. She dropped her head in her hands and sobbed. Ghita wavered, uncertain.

'That's not fair,' I said to her. 'We don't know Ed is guilty. David is the one who fancied Roz. He knew she was married, but that didn't stop him flirting with her.'

'But she knew I liked him. Why couldn't she let me have some fun for once? Why did she have to ruin everything?'

Lexi came over to the table.

'Ghita, dear, David was a monster. He chewed up women and spat them out, and he didn't care who he hurt. He did it to me, and to lots of other people I know. That man had no heart. He would have discarded you like a used tissue. There are many people who wanted him dead. Ed would have been at the back of the queue, even if David had dallied with Roz.'

'But David seemed so nice,' said Ghita, sniffing.

'His beauty was only skin deep,' I said. 'Underneath it lurked a philanderer who would have happily broken your heart.'

'I'm sorry,' said Roz. 'Ed has been impossible recently, and it made me unhappy. When David courted and flattered me, I felt normal again. It was thoughtless of me to ignore your feelings.'

'Don't think I forgive you,' said Ghita. 'Ed hasn't been proven guilty yet, but you played with us both just like David did. I'm not sure I want to be your friend anymore.'

She walked back into the office and shut the door. Roz gazed after her, stricken.

'This is such a nightmare,' she said. 'I don't think I could bear to lose Ghita. Do something. Please.'

I sighed.

'I can't bear to see you two fighting, but the police hold all the evidence. We'll have to work in the dark here. Do you know how David died?'

'No. They didn't tell me. Just that someone had stuffed him into the bulkhead once he was dead.'

'Well, one thing's for certain. Nobody could have carried him onto the boat alone, so either he died on board, or at least two people were involved in moving his body from somewhere else. I'll need to make a list of people with motives and work from there. Is there anything else I should know?'

Roz avoided my question by burying her face in her hands again. I got the distinct impression she knew more than she wanted to tell me, but I could winkle the information out of her later.

Meanwhile, I needed to find out who had called the Coastguard. How did the person who called in the crime know David's body had been hidden on board Ed's boat, if they hadn't placed it there themselves? And if they had murdered David, why call attention to themselves by revealing the presence of a body? If Ed had murdered David inside the cabin and taken him out to sea to throw him overboard, it seemed unlikely anyone else had seen the murder. I smelled a rat, and I had a secret weapon in this fight. A Mouse. My stepson and hacker par excellence. I wondered if I could distract him from Amanda's side long enough to do some detective work for me.

Chapter 10

The rift between Ghita and Roz only seemed to widen over the following days. I couldn't get any useful information from the police station as Flo, the Forensic consultant, and my not-so-secret source of leaked information, had taken her annual leave and disappeared to Egypt to work on some newly discovered mummies from a grave in the Valley of Kings. The scientists and archaeologists were hopeful of discovering how they had died by using the most modern forensic techniques. They had invited Flo to help them, so she went on a busman's holiday, dressed like an explorer from a bygone age, and wasn't due back for weeks. She, I could work with. We had a rather ad hoc friendship, but it survived our occasional forays into forbidden territory like titbits of information from the morgue. I didn't know her replacement, Donald Friske, but I knew George would have pre-warned him not to answer my questions.

Frustrated and saddened, I took the first opportunity to remove myself from the gloomy atmosphere at the shop and go with Harry on a clearance. He had received a call from a woman who lived in an old manor house in Little Stebbing, a village ten miles inland from Seacastle. She had asked him to come and revise the contents of a barn which had been used as an overflow for unwanted furniture for the last two hundred years. It sounded like a goldmine containing new stock for my shop. I still hadn't sold any of the taxidermy fish, nor had Lexi paid me for the one she had taken. She claimed to have mislaid the cheque, and I rued the day I missed the opportunity to get it from her. She promised to get another one the next time she went home. I needed the money, but I didn't need any extra tension in the shop, so I waited.

Harry turned up at the Grotty Hovel bright and early, and invited himself to breakfast. Mouse heard his voice and crawled out of bed to join us. Hades plonked himself on Harry's lap and purred like a steam engine, cocking a snoot at me. He still wouldn't let me stroke him without the danger of a nasty scratch. He seemed to take delight in random attacks when I had been lulled into a false sense of security. Since he had also saved my life, I put up with his antics, but he had earned his name. It started out as a joke while I thought up something better, but it stuck. Harry fed him little pieces of buttered toast, which he licked first and then crunched up, dropping crumbs on his fur. I put my tea into a travel cup and dragged Harry out to the van. Or we would have been there all day, chatting and eating with Mouse and Hades.

Harry's GPS led us deep into the West Sussex countryside, through picturesque villages with lawns of daisies, and past banks of late flowering primroses and daffodils on the shady side of the road. The trees were developing canopies of bright green leaves unfurling all along their branches. We left the windows open and the cool air of the late spring day made us both sigh in contentment. As the thickets of trees increased in density, their roots contained carpets of bluebells and their crowns had afros of blossom.

The roads narrowed to single lanes. They had had to install lay-bys to let oncoming traffic get by. To my delight, a mallard duck waddled across the road, followed by nine ducklings. Harry beamed at me.

'Can you imagine having nine children?' he said.

'Not really,' I said. 'I've only got one child, and he's eighteen and borrowed.'

Harry flashed me a sympathetic glance.

'I'm sorry. Was that thoughtless of me? Are you, um, were you, did you…'

I shrugged.

'George didn't want children. He said he'd done that already.'

'And you?'

'I've never been sure. He made all the important decisions in our house. I should have fought him over it, but when I got depression, it knocked the stuffing out of me. Anyway, my career kept me busy twenty-four-seven. How could I have managed children too?'

He nodded, but without conviction. With our usual barriers breached, I took my chance.

'What about you? Did you and Cathy plan to have any?'

He frowned.

'We tried without result for years. Then we thought she might finally be pregnant, but it turned out to be a tumour. Ovarian cancer. Stage four. A death sentence.'

My heart sank to the soles of my feet and I had to bite my lip hard to stop myself from crying.

'I'm so sorry,' I croaked. 'How awful for you both.'

'I tried to be strong for her, but my world fell apart and I started drinking to numb the pain. I thought I hid it well, but she knew. She always read me like a book.'

He swallowed.

'The day she died, she had half an hour of lucidity and talked to me for the last time despite the morphine haze. She made me promise to stop drinking and get on with my life.'

'And you have. She must be proud of you now.'

'Proud of me? She's gone. I hoped she would stick around for a while, but when I went home after the funeral, the house echoed like an empty stadium. She never came back to check on me or to comfort me. It's all a lie.'

A bitter edge had crept into his voice. What a pair we were. He longed for a ghost and me for my divorced husband. Neither of us had adjusted to our new realities.

We drove past a faded sign for the manor house. It took me a couple of seconds to react.

'That's the place. We just missed it.'

Harry swore under his breath. We had to drive nearly a mile before he found a suitable place to turn, a muddy gateway to a field full of grazing cattle. Harry needed me to open the gate in order to turn the van around. I jumped out and picked my way across the muddy ruts. The three-bar gate had a stiff bolt, but I forced it to slide across. I had to push the gate open and hold it while Harry backed into the gap. The van drove forward and sprayed my trousers with mud. I bent over to brush it off and I felt something bump into my rear end. A grumpy young bullock had objected to my presence in his field and trotted up to head butt me. I fell flat on my face in the muddy grass. Harry came running over and shooed the bullocks away. He offered me his hand and pulled me up. I staggered back to the van while he shut the gate, trying not to laugh. We got back into the van.

'I think that cow took offence,' he said, and giggled.

'He hedged his bets I couldn't fight back,' I said.

We started a battle of puns that lasted all the way up to the magnificent manor house. I couldn't stay cross with Harry for long, and mud dries fast. I didn't need to be clean to clear out a barn anyway.

Harriet Denby, the lady of the manor, came outside as we arrived and signalled us to go around the back. I would have liked to go through the house and take a peek at the inside of the medieval building, but maybe in my muddy state she would not have been welcoming. The barn ran the length of the backyard, parallel to the manor house. Its roof had sagged slightly in the middle, making the slates crack and break. We got out of the van and waited for her to greet us. Mrs Denby looked me up and down, and she sneered.

'There's the barn,' she said with a sweep of her arm. 'It's full of stuff. I don't suppose some of it has been seen for fifty years.'

I felt a frisson of excitement. Harry rubbed his chin.

'How do we do this?' he said.

'Why don't you divide it into two halves? Junk and serviceable? Then we can go through the better stuff and I'll give you prices on it.'

Harry looked unconvinced.

'We do clearance,' he said. 'I'm not an antique dealer. I remove unwanted furniture and pass it on to warehouses in London.'

'What about her? Didn't you say she was a dealer of some sort?' she said, gesturing at me. 'Can't she tell the difference between junk and antiques?'

I raised an eyebrow.

'*She* has a vintage shop,' I said.

Mrs Denby did not pick up my sarcasm.

'Get on with it then,' she said. 'I need this finished before my husband comes home.'

I could feel my blood boil at her attitude. As soon as she had shut the door of the manor house, I turned to Harry.

'Let's go home.'

He put his arm around my shoulders.

'You wouldn't make a very good soldier, you know. Surrendering at the first sight of the enemy is a little premature.'

'But she was so rude.'

'Hopefully, she is also stupid. You never know what we might find in here. Trust me.'

I shrugged.

'Lead on, officer.'

We opened the tall and wide double doors to the barn and stared in at the contents, which appeared untouched for years. Dusty cobwebs littered with the corpses of spiders, flies and wasps blanketed the furniture and dangled from the rafters. Despite my revulsion, I cleared them away. I wished I had brought some gloves, as I felt their crunchy bodies disintegrate under my touch. Harry saw my face and laughed. He grabbed an old broom and swept it back and forwards over the piles, twisting the cobwebs and dead insects into a giant, disgusting candy floss. He took it outside and chucked it on the ground.

'The junk goes here,' he said. 'And let's place anything decent over there.'

'Do you trust this woman?' I said. 'I have a feeling we're being played.'

He scratched his head.

'Now that you mention it, I think we need to be more strategic about our choices.'

'Why don't we put some vintage stuff we'd like in the junk pile? I'm pretty sure she doesn't know much about the value of anything and just wants her barn cleared out.'

'Okay, as long as she has the eventual choice, I don't see any harm. We'll offer to pay for it if she complains.'

We set to clearing the barn. Soon we were caked in dust and cobwebs despite Harry clearing the bulk out with his broom. Most pieces could be taken out by one person. I pointed left or right when Harry seemed unsure, mostly at the junk pile in the beginning. After a short while, we had a pile of broken chairs and chests with no drawers. I had seen no reasons to be cheerful so far, but I began to enjoy myself. The day was set fair, and the breeze had diminished. Bees buzzed in the wild flowers bordering the backyard. Harry took off his shirt, and I admired his well upholstered, still muscled torso. I was dying to ask him about his tattoo, but our earlier conversation had been intrusive enough for one day. I kept my thoughts to myself and just enjoyed the view. He loved physical exertion and whistled tunelessly, a sure sign the work appealed to him. I rolled up my sleeves and tied my shirt tails at my waist, glad of the cool air on my midriff.

The junk pile kept growing. It was thirsty work, and I peered through the back windows into the kitchen, hoping to catch Mrs Denby putting on a kettle. By chance, I spotted her making herself a pot of tea and tapped on the glass. She glanced over and I made a hand signal for drinking from a cup and grinned at her. If looks could kill, I would have dropped dead on the spot. However, she nodded and waved me away. About half an hour later, she brought out two cups of lukewarm tea in some old, chipped and stained mugs. Harry examined his with a jaundiced eye.

'These are definitely the cups she uses for the Help,' he said. 'You'd think she could've managed a biscuit.'

'They'd have been stale,' I said.

We went back to emptying the barn. I took great pleasure in taking a wee on her lawn, as I doubted she would offer to let me use her toilet. Harry laughed when I told him to stay in the barn so he wouldn't see me.

'You'll kill the grass,' he said.

'That's the plan.'

Just when I had given up, we found four Ercol cow horn chairs piled on top of each other. We put them on the pile of junk. Then Harry got my help to pull out a pair of scruffy, vintage French leather arm chairs which I put on the junk pile too, because I wanted them for the shop. Behind them, six wheelback dining chairs were stacked seat to seat beside an elm West Country Windsor armchair. They went on the good pile. A pair of vintage 1960s high stools with mid-century floral fabric made me squeak with delight, so I put them on the junk pile to test her taste. In the furthest corners of the barn, a couple of pretty oak bedside cabinets and a dresser with an adjustable mirror emerged from under a filthy tarpaulin. We stacked everything else decent on the right and congratulated ourselves on our labours. Mrs Denby must have been spying on us from the kitchen. As soon as we had finished, she materialised in the yard beside the 'good' pile and examined the contents.

'Can you give me a hand?' she said to Harry. 'I need to move those wheelback chairs into the kitchen.'

He shrugged at me in good humour and I watched in bemusement as she directed him to move the whole pile of excellent pieces either into the house or back into the barn. I even helped.

'Which pieces can we have?' I said, finally, knowing the answer already.

'I've decided to keep everything after all,' she said, smirking. 'But you can have the junk. Get a move on. My husband will be back soon and I want the yard cleared by then.'

She marched into the house and slammed the door. I caught Harry's eye, and he guffawed. I grimaced at the pain in my back.

'What a horrible old bat. She never intended to give us anything decent. She just used us to clear out her barn.'

'I suspected as much from the start,' he said. 'So that's why I put the Windsor armchair behind the French leather armchairs. And then there are your floral stools.'

'And the solid wood filing cabinet I put on the junk pile. It's an early Schreiber. I can get a hundred and fifty pounds for that from Grace, and she'll sell it for three hundred.'

'Let's put them in the van before Mrs Denby changes her mind.'

'She told us we could have them. She was so busy swindling us, she forgot to check the junk pile. I'd say it serves her right.'

'And what will you do with the actual junk?'

'I have no intention of taking that off her hands.'

As we drove off, I could see Mrs Denby emerge from her house to stare at the bonfire in the yard. Harry had salvaged a few pieces, but we didn't have any obligation to take the real junk with us. The tarpaulin acted as a great fire starter. Harry's face wore a smug expression.

'The war is never lost after the first battle,' he said. 'Let's celebrate with some Led Zeppelin.'

Chapter 11

Roz and I stood outside the coastguard's office in Pirate's Bay, looking out at the sea. The tide had come in sideways, driven by the strong westerly wind, and the water churned up the mud and silt trapped in the confines of the harbour. Thick grey water threw itself against the pier, draping the stanchions in seaweed. Herring gulls were grouped together on the shore, huddled against the chilly breeze. Ed's boat languished stranded at the pier, still draped in yellow plastic police tape, which formed streamers in the wind. Roz had moved back to their cottage, but I noticed the way she stared at the boat with longing. She and Ed loved to sleep there together, lulled by the waves.

We pushed open the door of the coastguard office and approached the desk. I had already agreed to let Roz do the talking. She claimed to have the man behind the desk under her spell and he certainly appeared mesmerised by her presence. He leaned across the desk and tried to touch her hair, but the look in her eyes would have scared Neptune. He backed off, and I read Pat Grady on his name badge. His rat-featured face registered fear and hope. He pushed his reading glasses back up his pointy nose.

'Roz, we rarely get the privilege of your company without that husband of yours.'

'He's otherwise engaged just now,' said Roz, batting her eyelashes at him.

'I don't know what you see in him, if I'm honest. There are plenty of better men around here who'd be willing.'

'Well, you might get the chance soon, because I hear you were manning the phones when the call came in.'

'What call would that be?'

'Don't act coy with me, Pat. You know which call I mean. Or aren't you willing anymore?'

Colour rose in his cheeks, emphasising his weather-beaten complexion.

'Oh, I'm still willing, but I shouldn't tell you. It would only cause ructions around here.'

'Why not? Ed's going to prison now. What difference will it make?'

'Because I know who made the call.'

I gasped despite myself.

'Who was it?' said Roz.

'I can't tell you. Like I told the police, a man with a hoarse voice.'

'Tell me.'

Pat shook his head.

'I'm no snitch. I could have told the police who called, but I pretended I didn't know.'

'Who asked you to tell the police? I'm want you to tell me.'

'I'm sorry, but I can't.'

Roz ran her fingers through her tangled mop of curls.

'Was it a fisherman?' she said.

'I can't say. But he said something odd.'

'What was that?'

'He told me we should search the boat for contraband. I don't think I've ever heard a dead body called that before. And—'

Roz held up her hand to silence him.

'We've got to go,' she said, and left, slamming the door behind her. I waved an apology at a disappointed Grady and followed her out.

'I don't think he had finished speaking,' I said. 'It could have been important.'

Roz shook her head.

'He's a self-important windbag. He just wanted to keep us there so he could flirt with me. I have a fair idea who the caller was, so there's something I need to show you.'

The breeze now carried rain, which fell in large cold drops on our heads and shoulders as we struggled to the beach huts along the shore to the east of Pirate's Bay. I wished I had worn my rain jacket as my clothes soaked it up and clung to me like jellyfish. The beach huts braced against one another on the shore, their paint faded to pastel and their doors padlocked until the summer. The wet sand clung to my shoes and crunched under my feet. Roz led me to one hut and selected a key from her bulging keyring. She shoved it into the padlock and jiggled it around until it clicked open. She removed it and put it in her pocket. I helped her shove the bar holding the door shut through the metal holders, and opened the door.

Once my eyes adjusted to the dim light inside the hut, I could see some rectangular packages wrapped in black plastic bags and sealed with masking tape. A smell I recognised filled the hut. I turned to Roz in consternation.

'Drugs?'

'No. Cigarettes. I saw someone taking them on board our boat the night of the murder.'

'David? Why on earth—'

'Not him. I have my suspicions about someone else, though. They say there's a roaring trade at the moment, and he has been taking advantage to bring in bundles from Europe.'

'But who would do that?'

Roz tapped the side of her nose.

'Do you remember who Ed had an argument with on the boat the day of the dive?' she said.

'David?'

'No, before that, with Len. They had a shouting match in the cabin on the way home.'

'What were they fighting about?'

'Ed told Len to stop smuggling cigarettes or he would report him. The fishermen don't want the council having any excuse to vote for the sanctuary. Len told Ed he needed the money because his catch had reduced so much.'

'But how did the cigarettes end up here?'

Roz sucked in her cheeks.

'I found them behind the bulkhead that night. I'm guessing Len planted them there to incriminate Ed. Then he made the call from a public telephone box reporting contraband on our boat.'

'But how did you know they were there?'

'I didn't. When I went on board that night, I noticed the bulkhead panel hanging open and I could see the packages inside. The panel doesn't stay shut once it's been opened, unless you close it correctly. You have to give it a sharp shove. I knew Ed wouldn't have had anything to do with smuggling, and besides, who puts packages on a boat before setting out to go fishing. It makes little sense.'

'So you removed them?'

'Yes. What else was I supposed to do?'

'Did you see David?'

Roz swallowed.

'No.'

'Or Len.'

'Neither of them. The cabin was empty.'

She avoided my inquiring glance. I felt like I had missed something.

'What were you doing there anyway? I thought Ed had planned to go fishing by himself.'

'David had asked to go with him. He wanted to get an idea of the catch size and the sizes of the individual fish.'

'And were you going to fish with them?'

'No, I, please don't ask me.'

'You'll have to tell the police about the smuggling and the fact you were on board that night.'

'Please, not yet. It will only complicate matters. We can find out who did it and tell the police.'

I rolled my eyes. George would kill me. And I wouldn't blame him.

'Okay, but as soon as we find a strong suspect, we go straight to the police.'

Chapter 12

It didn't take me long to regret my decision. As soon as I got home, my thoughts went into overdrive. If Roz had removed the cigarettes before Ed and David had got on board, who had killed David and placed him behind the bulkhead? I had the feeling Roz still hadn't told me everything. She had not explained what she had been doing on board in the first place, and that made me uncomfortable. She could also be a suspect, as Ed wasn't the only hothead in their household. Could she have done it? I found it hard to believe. She should tell George about the cigarettes, no matter what he read into it. I needed to persuade her as soon as I could.

I changed out of my wet clothes and jumped into my Mini car to drive through the rain to the shop. Luckily, I wore my raincoat and brought an umbrella, because I had to park so far from the shop I might as well have walked there. To my delight, Grace Wong had dropped in to negotiate with me over the Windsor chair. I had placed a bet with myself on the odds of her walking past more than once, before she had to come in and buy it. Grace and her husband Max were more colleagues than friends, but she made it to Ghita's Fat Fighter classes from time to time. Their antiques shop operated in another league to mine so we weren't exactly competitors, more like links in a chain. She looked around as the bell jangled and her face lit up.

'Tanya! How lovely to see you. I was just getting to know Mouse. He's such a gem.'

Mouse grinned. He always had the same effect on middle-aged women, being almost up to David's standards of handsome with similar Regency prince looks. I suppose I never dwelled on his appearance because he lived in my house as my unadopted son, a legacy of my ex-husband's intransigence. I shooed him upstairs 'so the grownups could negotiate'. Grace laughed.

'I never thought of you that way,' she said.

'Growing old is compulsory, growing up is not,' I said. 'I spent far too many years being an adult.'

'I wish I could be less adult sometimes. It's so tiring.'

She ran her hand over the top arc of the chair.

'Can I tempt you today?' I said, knowing full well she loved these chairs, and they sold like hot cakes from her shop. 'I've got some rather special taxidermy fish for you. Victorian with beautiful craftmanship.'

She wrinkled her nose at me.

'I'm sorry, but I think they're revolting. There's no way I'd have one of those monstrosities in my shop.'

'There's a great margin if you're interested.'

'No, thank you. But I would like this chair if you can bear to part with it.'

I certainly could. Harry and I had come to an agreement to go fifty-fifty on the profits of the things we extracted from Mrs Denby's barn. The Windsor chair would fetch a hefty sum if she put it in her window with a new coating of wax. I sighed theatrically.

'I'm not sure you can afford it, as I need to split the profit with Harry. It's not cheap.'

She smiled like a shark does before taking a bite out of a surfer.

'When are you going to introduce me to that man of yours? I'd love to meet him.'

I had zero intention of introducing her to Harry. She wanted to bypass me and make more money. I shook my head.

'He's mine, and I don't like to share. How much will you give me for the chair?'

She took my refusal well and paid me better. After she had left with Mouse who carried the chair for her, I stuffed the cash into the register with glee. Grace always carried around a seemingly endless supply of high value notes. She was asking to be mugged. I patted the case of one of the taxidermy fish and sighed. Why did nobody want them? Then I remembered Lexi's cheque. I mounted the stairs and knocked on their office door. Inside, Amanda prepared a presentation using the photographs from the dive with her head low over her laptop, and Lexi gesticulated at someone on the other end of her mobile phone call. I made us all a coffee using the machine and then knocked again to alert them.

Amanda came out almost immediately and slurped in appreciation as she drank hers.

'I'm going to miss this office when we go,' she said.

'When you go? Is Lexi planning on leaving?'

Lexi sat down beside me.

'Not yet,' she said. 'I would like to finish David's work here. We'd get a lot of kudos from success. It could generate tons of funding.'

'Would it?'

'Oh, yes. Success breeds success in this game. People jump on the bandwagon once it gets rolling. We might get celebrity endorsements too.'

'Maybe famous rock stars,' said Amanda.

'Which rock stars?' said Mouse, who had just got back from Grace's shop.

'Sting would be great,' said Lexi.

'Or Stormzy,' said Amanda.

'Who on earth is that?' said Lexi.

Mouse rolled his eyes at me.

'He's a rap artist,' he said.

'Oh, rap,' said Lexi. 'Not my thing at all.'

'Doesn't surprise me,' muttered Amanda.

'Stormzy is great,' said Mouse. 'I like his new gospel stuff.'

'Are you making progress identifying the fish from the photographs of the dive?' I said.

'We're almost finished,' said Amanda. 'Mouse is awesome at research.'

'We may have to steal him for our team,' said Lexi.

'Over my dead body,' I said, and then regretted it. 'By the way, Lexi, we haven't been to the Shanty yet. Do you fancy going for a drink tonight?'

'Are we invited too?' said Mouse.

'Sure, but I warn you, we'll be reminiscing about past times and you may be bored.'

'We don't have to sit with you,' said Amanda. 'I'd like to go. I hear there is a wonderful view from there.'

'It sounds like fun,' said Lexi. 'But let's not wear the same outfit.'

I smiled.

'It's a deal. We can go straight from here after work.'

While the others returned to the office, I went downstairs and made a list of the suspects in the murder and their motives. As far as I could make out, anybody could have boarded Ed Murray's boat on the night of David's murder. Could Len have returned with more cigarettes and killed David by mistake? Had someone made an appointment to meet David on the boat? What about Roz? She wasn't telling me the truth about that night. She shut down Pat Grady at the coastguard's office when he seemed about to tell us something else. Did she do that on purpose?

It would help to know how David had died, but Flo hadn't returned from her holiday yet, so I couldn't ask her to find out. If he had been killed by a blow to the back of the head, it could have been a case of mistaken identity, or even an accident. David and Ed were both tall with short hair. What if someone intended to kill Ed, but got David in error in the dark? David had a long list of enemies because of his philandering, but Ed also had his detractors. What about the other stakeholders in the talks? Frank Burgess had threatened violence in the meeting we held when David was already dead, and he had claimed to be dealing with the problem. Was the problem David? And then there was Marion Pocock, but what motive could she have besides resenting him? Even

Lexi and Amanda seemed to have motives for killing David, but not Ed.

I decided we needed to do some research into Frank Burgess. On the surface, he appeared to have a powerful motive to prevent the establishment of the sanctuary. But his business had a Shoreham address. Why did he care about Seacastle? Mouse had his hands full helping Lexi, and she paid him far more than I could afford, so I did my own digging. The skills I had honed as an investigative journalist held me in good stead despite my struggles with modern technology, and I had learned to use a browser to search for information from Mouse. I carried out my search at home so as not to upset the apple cart. I didn't want Lexi getting involved. My spider senses told me Frank Burgess was hiding something and I couldn't wait to find out what.

Chapter 13

I parked the Mini as close as I could to the Shanty, but we still had to walk the rutted path along the cliffs from the car park to the ancient pub. It perched high above Pirate's Bay and had a fabulous view of the wind farm far out to sea. The evenings were getting brighter as we headed for summer, and the wind turbines stood white against the skyline. A massive tanker headed past them for Holland or Germany. Ed's boat was still lashed to the pier below us, the remains of the police tape not visible, but present. I couldn't help being drawn to the scene. Roz and Ghita were my closest friends. I had to keep us all together somehow.

'Do you think Ed did it?' said Mouse.

I turned to look at him and observed his bright blue eyes fill with concern as his black curls whipped in the wind. I pulled him closer with an arm around his shoulders and he did not resist.

'Of course not, sweetheart, but your father is an experienced officer, so we need to have faith in his judgement on this one.'

Lexi snorted.

'Of course he did it. Jealousy is a powerful motive and Roz couldn't help herself where David was concerned.'

'You don't know that,' said Mouse. 'You were jealous too. I saw you looking at them talking. You hate Roz.'

'Don't be ridiculous. You're just a child. What do you know?'

'More than you think,' muttered Mouse.

Amanda pushed past us.

'Come on,' she said, grabbing Mouse's hand. 'We all need to grow up. There's nothing any of us can do right now.'

I slipped my arm into Lexi's.

'Forget it. We're all on edge after what happened,' I said.

Amanda and Mouse had stopped to look at the notice board outside the Shanty. A garish poster proclaimed the appearance of famed local Frank Sinatra tribute, Lance Emerald. For one night only. I sighed. I had never heard of him, and Joy liked to give everyone one chance at fame.

'We should have worn matching outfits after all,' said Lexi. 'I've a feeling it's going to be a long night.'

'Fingers and toes crossed,' I said.

Excitement leaked out of The Shanty as we approached the tiny door characteristic of coastal properties. Ryan Wells, Joy's husband and a bit of a boffin, told me the small size kept the heat in, but I blamed the window tax of King William III. A fair-sized crowd had invaded the pub by the time we struggled through the tiny door, but Mouse spotted an unoccupied corner table at the window seat, and surged forward to grab it. We all squeezed onto the padded banquettes and signalled to Shaylah, Ryan's barmaid, to come and clear the table, which had already been covered with dirty bottles and glasses. She gave Mouse a long stare, but he showed no sign of noticing. Amanda sent her a laser-like glare, marking her territory in no uncertain fashion, and Shaylah shook her hair in defiance.

'What can I get you ladies?' she said, chewing morosely on her pen, and stealing more sidelong glances at Mouse through her false eyelashes.

'I'll have a gin and tonic,' said Lexi. 'Which gins do you stock?'

'I don't know.'

'Any sort is fine. Gordons perhaps?'

Normally, I prefer a cider, but I put up two fingers.

'And the children?' said Shaylah.

I guffawed.

'They're both over eighteen,' I said. 'They can tell you themselves.'

As Shaylah wiggled away to get our drinks, Ryan rang the ship's bell at the bar and held up his hands for silence. He had raised the seat of his wheelchair to its fullest extent, so he looked like Yoda hovering over the bar.

'Silence please,' he said. 'I have great pleasure in introducing Lance Emerald, Seacastle's foremost Frank Sinatra tribute, back to live among us after an enforced absence of many years, with a selection of favourites from the Golden Age of Crooners.'

I noticed his careful use of language and I wondered what had caused Lance's enforced absence. Prison? Joy could be soft-hearted, so some acts she hired were pretty ropey. Lance himself looked far past his prime. He appeared unsteady on his feet and kept taking his packet of cigarettes out of his pocket and then replacing them again. I wondered if he had been somewhere that they allowed smoking in pubs. Then he lifted a boombox into the bar and put on a tape.

'At least you've got CDs,' said Mouse, smirking at me. 'This guy's equipment is also from the golden age of the crooners.'

Lance coughed twice, a racking, phlegmy sound, and then he tapped the microphone, causing it to screech. I covered my ears with my hands.

'Make it stop,' I said.

'Keep your hands there. He's about to sing,' said Lexi.

'I wish I'd brought ear plugs,' said Amanda.

But we were all wrong. Lance had a couple of false starts, which made the crowd uneasy and silent with embarrassment, but then he hit his straps. Song after song filled the bar with beloved songs from Old Blue Eyes in his prime. I closed my eyes and I could hear the same phrasing and timing. All too soon, Lance had finished his set. Everyone in the bar joined in an explosive round of applause. Lance lapped it up. I notice him scouring the crowd like an eagle hovering over a colony of rabbits, looking for easy prey. His gaze settled on Mouse and with unexpected speed he made his way to our table.

'Lance Emerald,' he said, addressing Mouse. 'And you are?'

'Andrew Carter,' said Mouse, leaning away from the wrinkled face shoved across the table. I knew the use of his real name was a signal he felt uncomfortable.

'Andy. How nice. Maybe you'd like me to buy you a drink?'

'No, he wouldn't,' I said.

'And who are you?'

I puffed my chest out.

'I'm his mother.'

The startled expressions around me almost made me laugh. Lance sneered.

'Can't he tell me himself?'

Mouse, who had been shaking with annoyance, turned and kissed Amanda hard. I don't think she expected such a bold move, but she joined in with gusto.

'For heaven's sake. Get a room you two,' said Lexi, flapping her hands.

Lance's upper lip curled. Then he flounced off to the toilets. I watched him go. Then I noticed Ryan beckoning me from the bar, so I excused myself and slid between the tables to get there.

'I see you've met Lance Emerald,' he said. 'I apologise. He is a superb singer, but a predatory little shit.'

'It takes all types,' I said. 'David de Frontenac, the head of the Kelp Sanctuary project, had the same problem, but he only targeted women.'

'I heard about his murder. I wonder who got their own back,' said Ryan. 'Will Mouse be okay? Lance isn't fussy about their sex, but he prefers them barely out of puberty.'

'Mouse can look after himself. I have wondered if the motive for killing David could be jealousy, but there seem to be many possibilities, including mistaken identity.'

'Are they sure that someone murdered him, and he didn't die in an accident?'

I shrugged.

'I don't know for sure yet. My source has deserted me and gone to Egypt.'

'I don't know if the Egyptians are ready for Flo,' he said, grinning. 'Can't you ask George?'

'In theory I could, but he has warned me not to get involved.'

'It makes sense. You're not exactly a neutral party on this one.'

I sighed.

'That makes it even harder to ignore. I don't suppose you worked that night?'

'I had some business to attend to. Joy took the helm.'

Questions surged to my lips, but I held my silence. We were all quite convinced Ryan had worked for MI5 or MI6, and no one could agree if he still did or not. He and Joy took over the pub after he became a paraplegic. They turned up in Seacastle out of the blue and took over the Shanty, becoming fixtures overnight as they transformed the pub from a filthy dive into a cosy and welcoming haven up on the cliffs.

'Where is she tonight?'

'She's busy.'

No wonder we thought they were both spies.

'Will she be back soon?'

'Probably tomorrow.'

Lexi and Amanda took a cab back to their guesthouse, and I drove Mouse to the Grotty Hovel. I thought he would stay with Amanda, but he whispered in her ear and gave her a peck on the cheek before getting back into the Mini. I waited for him to say something about the evening. He twisted his hands in his lap and looked out of the window. I could almost feel the effort it took for him to stay silent. When we got home, I put on the kettle while he sat on the sofa cuddling Hades. As I poured the water into my cup, he came to the door of the kitchen with Hades still in his arms. Time stood still for an instant.

'You told Lance Emerald that you're my mother,' he said.

I froze. What an idiot thing to say. I hadn't planned it.

'I did,' I said, without turning around. 'He was out of order. I wanted to protect you.'

I waited for an answer, but none came. Instead, I heard Hades' claws click on the kitchen floor and I felt Mouse's arms snake around me. I twisted to face him and held him tight, trying to control the surge of emotion.

'I'm sorry,' I whispered. 'I know I'm a pretty poor substitute. And you're all grown up. But—'

'I love you too,' he said.

Chapter 14

I got up early the next morning because I wanted to be the first to arrive at the shop. I couldn't take the chance of Ghita and Roz turning up and having another row with no referee. Hades demanded I open the back door for him when I got downstairs. I bent down and tried to push him through the cat-flap, but he wriggled free and yowled until I opened the door. Ratbag! Someone knocked on the front door as I shut the back door. I pulled it open, expecting the postie with a parcel or a registered delivery, but George stood there in his overtight suit. His increase in weight made him self-conscious, but I thought he carried it well. I congratulated myself on my taste.

'Did the post office go on strike again?' I said.

'Hilarious. Can I come in?'

'Do I have a choice?'

'Not really. Any chance of some breakfast? Sharon has me on a diet and I'm starving. I could kill a fry-up.'

'How about a compromise? I will boil you a couple of eggs if you like?'

'If you make me some soldiers.'

I couldn't help smiling. George loved nursery food. His grandmother had cooked for him when he was a little boy, and his taste in food hadn't become any more sophisticated since. When we were married, I used to disguise onions and garlic in our food by liquidising them. He used to tell everyone he hated garlic, but I knew better. He sat at the table in the kitchen and watched me make a pot of tea and take stuff out of the cupboards. I set the egg timer for soft yolks. I boiled an egg for myself too. George hated to eat alone.

'Are you going to tell me why you're here?' I said. 'Apart from the hunger pangs.'

George took off the top of his egg with a precise swipe of his spoon. He stuck a soldier of toast into the yolk and munched it in one bite.

'Correct me if I'm wrong, but I heard you and Roz visited the coastguard's office together. Do you want to tell me what you were doing there?'

I played for time by buttering my toast.

'We might have.'

'Did you learn anything new?'

I sighed.

'I did, but not from the coastguard.'

George ate another soldier.

'And are you going to tell me about it?'

I looked him straight in the eye.

'Do you have an open mind about the murder? I mean, you have access to the autopsy and I don't so—'

'Tell me what you know.'

I told him about Len and the cigarettes. His eyes opened wider, but he continued to eat his breakfast without comment.

'Roz thinks Len rang the coastguard to report Ed's contraband cargo.'

'Does she now?'

George rubbed his chin with his napkin, removing a blob of yolk.

'It may interest you to know that some kids fooling around on their bikes saw Len using the old phone box. They remembered it clearly because usually people use it as a urinal and they had never seen anyone actually make a call before. They called him a fossil, but he shuffled off trying to hide his face.'

'Is he a suspect?'

'Of what? Trying to nobble a rival? Possibly. But why would he murder David?'

'Maybe to stop the sanctuary?'

George ran his fingers through his mop of hair. I could see silvery glints which hadn't been there before.

'Did Ed tell you David had asked to go fishing with him?' I said.

'He did.'

'They must look similar from behind in the gloomy cabin. How do you know David was the intended target?'

'I don't. The autopsy hasn't been carried out yet, and I didn't get a good look at the body. We think he died of a blow to the head, but I'm not allowed near the corpse until Flo does her magic.'

'Flo? What about Donald Friske?'

'Angina.'

'That's a blow.'

'She's back soon. I can't narrow down the motives until I know if the person who killed him did it from behind or in front.'

'Will you release Ed?'

'I already have. We couldn't keep him any longer without charging him.'

'Roz must be thrilled.'

'I suppose she is. I'd better pay a visit to Len and ask him some questions.'

'Roz has the key to the beach hut, if you need it.'

'I'll get her back in to the station. Do you know what she was doing on the boat? Did she plan to go fishing with them?'

I shook my head.

'She didn't say,' I said, looking at my watch and trying not to appear nervous. 'I've got to go to work.'

George raised an eyebrow, but he didn't press me. Instead, he helped me to clear up the breakfast, something he had never done when we were married.

'I see Sharon has domesticated you,' I said, grinning.

'She's a lot stricter than you were. It's different.'

He sighed.

'But you're happy?' I said.

He shrugged.

'She hasn't heard of the films I like. And she's put me on a diet. I'm not allowed any of the foods I want to eat.'

I should have been pleased, but I felt sorry for him. George had simple needs, which I always fulfilled without fuss, because it kept him happy. I often wondered what would have happened to us if I hadn't become ill. We never fought before then, and we had a lot in common. I patted him on the bottom.

'Go on, get out of here. If I hear anything important, I promise to let you know.'

He slapped his forehead.

'I nearly forgot. Ed told me everyone on the dive trip had a camera with them. Can you round up the memory cards for me?'

'They're in the office. But they've been touched by everyone lots of times.'

'Not for the fingerprints. I need to examine their contents in case we can gather any clues to the motives for murder.'

'I'll ask Mouse to get them to you this morning.'

'Thanks darling. I mean, Tan.'

He bent down and kissed my cheek, lingering for an instant longer than necessary. I shut the door behind him, flushed with a weird excitement. I knew him pretty well. He had not done anything that intimate for years.

'Who was that?'

Mouse stood at the foot of the stairs, rumpled with sleep.

'Your father.'

'Dad? What did he want?'

'Breakfast.'

Chapter 15

I relayed George's request for the memory cards to Mouse, and when we got to the shop, he went straight to the office and collected them from his desk drawer. Amanda had separated them in tiny Ziplock bags with the owner's names on them, and put all of them into one bag marked camera chips. We tipped them out onto a table and went through them one by one.

'There's no card for David,' I said.

'Didn't he use his phone?' said Mouse. 'He showed me a fancy case he had for using it underwater.'

'That's right. I remember now. But where's his phone?' I said. 'Can you ask George if they have it at the station? Presumably he had it on him when he died.'

'Will do.'

'Okay, see you later.'

Mouse hadn't been gone long before Ghita made a sheepish appearance. She wrung her hands together and could hardly look me in the eye. I didn't help her through the awkward moment.

'Oh, Tanya, what must you think of me? I'm such a fool. And poor Roz. Will she ever speak to me again? I'm a rubbish friend.'

She sobbed on my shoulder until it became quite damp. I didn't bother to respond. Amanda looked down at us and caught my eye. I signalled for her to put on the kettle. I could see why Mouse liked her. We had little in common, but she had a kind heart and Hades liked her, according to Mouse. Hades represented the acid test for anyone who came to the house. The fact he still steered clear of me made me sad, but he associated me with his incarceration in a laundry basket in his former home. Forget elephants, cats have longer memories.

Once we were ensconced upstairs, Ghita confessed she had heard about Ed being set free. I didn't bother to enlighten her on the regulations for releasing a suspect if he hadn't been charged. Nor did I mention the fact that both he and Roz were still very much in the frame as potential suspects. I needed Ghita onside, both for Roz's sake and the investigation. As always, Ghita perked up after her cup of tea. I hoped it had not refilled her tear ducts.

'George came to see me this morning,' I said.

'How exciting! Does he want you back?'

I tutted in irritation.

'No, about the case.'

'Oh. What did he say?'

'He told me David's autopsy has not been carried out yet, because they don't have a pathologist available. Flo is due back from Egypt next week, but so far the cause of death hasn't been established.'

'It can't be an accident. Why would someone hide him in the bulkhead if so? Surely they'd just call an ambulance?'

'But what if they had a powerful motive and panicked in case the police didn't believe them? We have a list of suspects as long as your arm.'

'I know all the opponents of the sanctuary are suspects, but who else is there?'

'David had a reputation as a philanderer. What if a jealous husband or a slighted woman got their revenge? The pier is quiet at night. It would have been easy to lie in wait for David on Ed's boat.'

'But how did they know he would be there?'

I pursed my lips.

'An excellent question, my dear Watson.' I took out my notebook. 'We need to find out who knew David would leave on the boat with Ed.'

'I think that might be a short list. What if he didn't tell anyone?'

I knew one person on that list, but I didn't mention her.

'Which suggests that maybe he wasn't the intended victim. Lots of people may have known Ed would be on his boat,' said Ghita.

'The other fishermen, the members of the stakeholders' committee.'

'Wait. How did they know?'

'Ed sent a round robin email to see if anyone wanted to come fishing at night, but it seems only David turned up. Well, David and his murderer, if it wasn't Ed. I need a reason to question them.'

Ghita shrugged.

'You're a journalist. People love to talk about themselves. Just pretend you are interviewing the people involved in the tragedy in order to write an article about the sanctuary.'

I would try out her theory by calling Frank Burgess. If he had intended to intimidate me, he did an excellent job at the council meeting with his veiled threats about David. George had dismissed him as a suspect for now, but the fact he had turned up to the stakeholder's meeting meant he had something to lose if the sanctuary went ahead. He had claimed inside information about David, but I found it hard to believe that murdering him could have been the solution he had in mind. Harry had muttered something about him being all feathers and no beak, but I wasn't so sure.

As Ghita had predicted, Burgess's own self-importance blinded him to the real reason for the interview and he accepted with alacrity. I got hold of Harry, who agreed to come with me in case of trouble. We drove to Shoreham along the coast road, admiring the flat sands with their scattered rock pools draped in brown seaweed. Herring gulls called and swooped over the people enjoying a walk along the promenade. Brighton shimmered in the distance, flanked by cliffs of white chalk. We crossed the estuary into Shoreham and found parking in a back street lined with trees in full blossom. I kicked at the petals as we walked along, sending them into the air and making pink rain. Frank Burgess's office sat over a chippy and the aroma of vinegar followed us up the shabby staircase to where a pretty woman with wavy brown hair sat behind a basic desk set up with a Dell desktop and printer in front of her. She peered around the side of her screen.

'Visitors,' she said. 'There's not much call for them around here.'

But she smiled at Harry, batting her eyelashes at him like a shy schoolgirl. He glanced around him in embarrassment, so I distracted her by asking if we could go straight in.

'Oh yes, he's waiting for you, Ms Bowe.' She turned to Harry. 'You'll have to wait out here I'm afraid. He's not expecting you. Frank doesn't like surprises.'

Her attitude got right up my nose and I didn't like the way her eyes devoured Harry. I considered protesting, but Harry shook his head and flicked his eyes at the receptionist, indicating he would question her while I tackled Frank. I rolled my eyes at him, but he had already pulled a chair up to her desk.

'Harry,' he said, putting out his hand.

'Emily. Please to meet you.'

More eyelash action. I almost guffawed, but the inner office door opened and Frank Burgess stood there in a shiny suit. I suspected he had dressed up for his interview.

'Hello, Mr Burgess,' I said. 'Shall we get started?'

He beamed and guided me into his office with a hand on the small of my back, which felt alarmingly close to my bottom. I strode in ahead of his touch and sat on a leather couch, hoping he wouldn't join me there. I watched him calculating my reaction to such a move, but he plumped for the worn armchair in matching brown leather. He settled himself into his seat and undid the button of his suit jacket, which threatened to fly across the room because of the pressure it was under.

'What do you want to know?' he said.

'Can we start with a quick portrait of your business, how you got started and what you do from day to day?' I said.

He cleared his throat. A loud peal of girlish laughter rang out from Emily's office, making us both bristle with annoyance. I took out my mobile phone.

'Is it okay if I record you?'

Frank's focus returned to me. He waved his hand magnanimously and then launched into a long and involved description of his deprived childhood and how he had been wronged by people who would pay for it one day. I wondered if David had been added to that list. As Frank expounded on his career, I took a long look around his office. The brown walls were decorated with photographs of dredgers and their crews, and the shelves behind his desk were covered with curios, which I suspected resulted from mud larking in the Thames as a boy. I longed to examine them, but I didn't want to irritate him by breaking the flow of his reminiscences. He appeared to be finishing, and I smiled in approval.

'That's some story. You should write a book.'

'My friends always say that. I don't suppose…'

I laughed.

'Afraid not. Only newspaper and magazine articles.'

'You're wasted on them. What does your husband think?'

That old chestnut. But I disappointed him.

'He encouraged me of course,' I said, wishing it had been true. George had always resented my work; despite the freedom it gave us from financial worries and the top class holidays we could afford. I wondered how Sharon felt when she discovered how little he earned, and how much our comfortable lifestyle had depended on my income. Another peal of laughter brought me back to the present.

'Can you tell me how the sanctuary will affect your business?'

'It's a disaster. I'm totally against it. Bleeding-heart environmentalists are going to ruin me.'

'Did you hear what happened to David de Frontenac?'

'That prat? I could tell you a thing or two about that sham operator.'

'Haven't you heard?' I said. 'David's dead. Murdered.'

Frank Burgess's jaw dropped with a metaphorical clang. Then he sat back in his chair, shaking his head.

'I knew he'd get his comeuppance one day, but I never expected...'

He tailed off. His surprise seemed genuine.

'You didn't know about it?'

'Of course not. I don't like your tone. Are you suggesting—'

'Absolutely not.' I needed to say something to distract him. 'I couldn't help noticing the photograph on your desk.'

'What photograph?' He spun around to look at the photograph of him and the young woman. He slapped his head and smirked. 'I meant to take that down. You got me there.'

'Marion Pocock was your girlfriend?'

'My sister.'

'Don't you think you should have revealed that in the stakeholder meeting? She is hardly a neutral party to the debates.'

'The sanctuary will ruin me if I don't stop it,' said Burgess. 'But I'm not a murderer. That man was a fraud and I reckon his past caught up with him.'

'How do you know he was a fraud?'

'Takes one to know one. There was something not entirely kosher about our Mr F.'

His voice betrayed an admiration I hadn't heard before. Maybe dying had that effect on people.

'Do you have any evidence?'

He stood up.

'I don't have any more to say to you today. You've got your interview. I'd like you to leave now.'

I nodded.

'Thank you for your time. I hope you find a solution to your problems.'

He grunted and opened the door. I spotted Harry leaning in to gaze at Emily's chest. He snapped back when he saw me, guilt on his face.

'Oh, hi Tanya. Emily was just showing me her—'

'I noticed. Shall we go? I've got what I came for.'

'Um, I'm taking Emily to lunch. You can come if you want to or…'

I sighed.

'I'll take the bus. See you later.'

He gave me an apologetic grin, and a smirk crossed Emily's face. I had hated her on sight, and now I knew why.

Chapter 16

Harry's lunch date with Emily made me more than a little jealous. Rightly or wrongly, I thought of him as mine, but our relationship had stuttered to a halt due to the fear of ruining our friendship. Now neither of us knew how to restart it. When he arrived at the shop, beaming and brimming over with news, I pretended I didn't care about being stood up. Instead, I offered him a coffee and carried on as usual. He sat upstairs with me and Mouse, and I told him about the interview with Frank Burgess.

'So that's what he meant about friends in high places,' said Harry. 'Isn't having a sister on the council a conflict of interests?'

'I'll have a word with Ghita. She can let Marion know we're on to her. It doesn't mean he's innocent, though. What's his motive for interfering with the establishment of an MPA in Seacastle when he lives in Shoreham?' I said.

'Emily says Frank is in trouble,' he said. 'He's got some pending court cases.'

'Is that in Shoreham?' said Mouse. 'I can find out what's going on.'

He opened his laptop and started tapping the keys. Harry looked peeved. I guessed he didn't want his scoop bettered.

'Go on.' I said.

'Well, Emily says he can't release silt offshore at Shoreham anymore, because they caught him dumping some onto the scallop beds.'

Emily says, Emily says. Ha!

'I've found the court case,' said Mouse.

'Emily says he has been coming up the coast to unload silt offshore at Seacastle,' said Harry.

I think I'd like to stab Emily.

'But if they ratify the imposition of the Marine Protected Area, he'll have to take the silt miles offshore. It will ruin his business,' I said.

'He's also been done for selling beach sand to builders,' said Mouse.

'Why is that bad?' I said.

'It adulterates the cement,' said Harry. 'It causes it to crumble and age much quicker due to the salt.'

'Did Emily tell you that?' I said, trying not to sound sarcastic.

'No, I already knew,' said Harry, and he gave me a funny look.

I felt like my heart had fallen out of my chest. My jealousy over Emily now threatened to ruin my future with Harry. I couldn't tell you why. I'm supposed to be intelligent, but romance has always turned me into a fool. Mouse hadn't noticed the atmosphere, and he prattled on about financial jeopardy being a powerful motive for murder. I had to force my attention back to the case.

'We need to find out why Burgess thinks David had a dodgy past. Does he actually know something or is it just suspicion based on his dislike of David's posh origins?'

'I could ask Emily if you like. We're going to the talk on military installations along the coast on Tuesday.'

I swallowed a rebuke. I doubted Emily had an interest in pill boxes, but I could see why she would pretend.

'Great idea. She is bound to have important information.'

I hadn't meant my tone to convey sarcasm, but I caught Mouse staring at me for a second. Then he looked away and went back to tapping on the laptop. Harry and I finished our coffee in silence before he left. He gave me a cheery wave, but I sensed a subtle shift, one I hadn't expected. It made me feel wretched.

I had hoped to go to the Shanty with Harry and have a cosy chat with Joy Wells, but his obvious interest in Emily had hurt my feelings. Instead, I drove by myself to the carpark in the Mini and fought the westerly breeze to the door of the pub. I let myself in and looked around. Two regulars sat in our window seat nattering. I recognised one of them as Bert Higgins, Ed Murray's friend who had come to the Second Home on that first day with Roz and David. I had not considered him to be on my list of suspects. He had come on the dive, but not to the council meeting, so seemed to be a follower rather than a leader as far as the sanctuary went. I listened for a while and picked up comments about tides and nets and new-fangled fishing technology, but nothing about the kelp sanctuary. Many people had presumed, wrongly, that David's death would be the end of the project.

I chose a stool at the bar under the glass float collection, which rivalled the one I now had at Second Home. Joy came out from the back and her eyes raked over me like an x-ray scanner at the airport.

'I didn't know you were here,' she said. 'The lager barrel needed changing.'

She didn't look strong enough to change a barrel, but appearances can be deceptive. Joy had sinewy arms and legs, which often imply strength.

'No problem. I love it in here when it's empty.'

'I don't. No money in that. Come to drown our sorrows, have we?' she said.

I couldn't help laughing.

'Actually, I came to interrogate you, but I guess you're used to that.'

Did I imagine it, or did a shadow flit across her face? I wished I could ask her more about her past. Maybe I'd catch her on a day when she relaxed her guard.

'Ryan? Yes, he's a bit like the Spanish Inquisition. I'll answer your questions if you tell me why you're carrying the weight of the world on your shoulders.'

I shrugged.

'It's not so important.'

'A burden shared is a burden halved.'

'It's Harry,' I said. 'I think I've driven him into the arms of another woman.'

She raised an eyebrow.

'I thought you two were just friends. Although I could never imagine why. That man is a catch.'

'Apparently someone else thinks so too.'

'What happened?'

'He took Frank Burgess's secretary out to lunch. Supposedly to find out about Frank's interest in the sanctuary, but I didn't like the way they were flirting.'

'Aren't you jumping the gun a little? They're not getting engaged, just having lunch.'

'You're right. And I don't blame him for getting distracted. We had an agreement, but…'

Did we really? Or had he backed off because I couldn't make my feelings clear?

'Maybe he got lonely waiting for you to be ready. Everyone knows you still hold a candle for George,' said Joy.

Was I so transparent? Did everyone know? Even George?

'I can't believe I screwed this up so badly.'

'Maybe you and George need to have a chat? Clear the air? Dot the 'I's and cross the 'T's. Then you and Harry can give it a proper go.'

Maybe. I sighed and leaned my chin on my hand.

'Want a half of cider?' said Joy.

'Yes, please. And a packet of salt and vinegar crisps.'

'That's my girl. Now, what did you want to ask me about?'

'David de Frontenac. Ryan told me you were working at the bar the night he died.'

'Ah, I was afraid you might ask me about that.'

She pulled up a stool and served herself tonic water with a slice of lemon. I waited. Joy does not like to be rushed. She wiped a strand of hair from her face and took a sip of her drink.

'Ask away,' she said.

'How much do you know about David's death?' I said.

'More than I should. You know how people talk after a few drinks.'

And she tilted her head towards the two locals in the corner.

'Like what?'

'I heard about Len and the cigarettes. He's an unsavoury piece of work. Did you know he came here the night David died?'

'No, I didn't. Do you remember what time that was?'

'Just before ten o'clock. I remember because David asked me for the time.'

'David was here that night too?'

'Yes. He left shortly before Len got here. I think they may even have met at the door. I had my hands full though, with Ryan away, so I can't swear to it.'

'When did Len leave?'

'I'm not sure. Before last orders, I think.'

'Did you notice Ed's boat setting off from Pirate's Bay?'

'Yes, it sailed out as I shut up the pub. I remember being surprised as he usually moves out with the high tide. He left later that night.'

'Maybe he was waiting for someone? But didn't you say David left here before ten? They were going to the fishing grounds together.'

'It wouldn't have taken more than ten minutes to get to the harbour. Why did it take them so long to set sail once David got there?'

Joy shrugged.

'Something is weird about this. Are we sure the target was David? He reminded me a little of Ed in build. Also, Ed's no fool. I don't see him killing David on his boat. It makes little sense.'

'I've been thinking the same thing. I haven't crossed Len off my list of suspects yet. I'm desperate for Flo to get back so I can find out how David died,' I said.

'Is she still on holiday? She's back any minute, I think.'

Joy took a long swig of her drink and crunched an ice cube between her teeth.

'There's something else,' she said. 'Something I didn't tell George. Well, he didn't ask me.'

'What about? Did you see something from up here?'

Joy rubbed her face, stalling. I let her decide.

'Not long before the boat left, I noticed someone walking down the street to the pier, someone I thought I recognised.'

'Wasn't it too dark?'

'She walked under the streetlamp.'

'She?'

'Someone wearing a floaty dress with blonde curly hair.'

'Roz? But I thought she went home after leaving the cigarettes in the beach hut?'

'That's what she told you. But rumour has it, she and David were having a fling.'

I frowned.

'Not that I know of. But he flirted with her all the time and she lapped it up. You know Roz.'

Joy nodded, but I could sense the cogs whirring. They mirrored the ones in my head.

'What if something went wrong between them? Have you asked her what happened that night?'

'She's definitely hiding something. When the police arrested Ed, she told me it was her fault. But she wouldn't elaborate. She told me she had found Len's cigarettes, but not what happened afterwards,' I said.

'It sounds like you need to talk to her before I tell the police about seeing her on the pier.'

'Thanks Joy. I will.'

We finished our drinks. I fancied another, but I remembered I had brought the Mini with me, so I kissed her and promised to keep her posted on the latest news of the case. The wind had picked up, and it blew me along the path to the carpark. I had gone to the Shanty hoping for evidence about who murdered David, but now I had a suspect I hadn't expected.

Oh Roz. What have you done?

Chapter 17

On my way home, I received a text from George asking if he could pop in and talk about the case. Normally I would have been thrilled that he deigned to discuss his work with me, and so soon after his last visit, but I knew I would have to spill the beans about Roz. I dreaded his reaction. Roz had never been welcomed in our house while we were married. I had to meet both her and Ghita at Fat Fighters, as he didn't approve of me seeing either of them.

'What's wrong with my friends? You can't go wrong with police officers,' he used to say.

And now she had put herself in the frame for murder, I found it hard to disagree. When I didn't reply immediately, he sent a second text.

'Indian or Chinese?'

I knew Mouse had a date with Amanda at some local gig, and my stomach rumbled at the thought of a curry, so I texted him back – Indian, please. Chicken korma and poppadoms.

We met on the doorstep of the Grotty Hovel. George's face flushed with the triumph of a hunter bringing home his kill as he held out the bag of hot food. I couldn't help grinning. We used to have curry evenings in, when we were first married. We'd watch a movie, always his choice, because I couldn't bear his running commentaries on my romantic comedies and cosy mysteries. I opened the door, almost tripping over Hades who made a beeline for the cat flap. I remembered I hadn't told George the truth about Hades. When he had questioned me before, I told him I was fostering Hades and had given him back. I knew he wouldn't approve, so when he didn't spot Hades, I didn't comment. George sat at the table in the kitchen while I found us some plates and utensils. I put extra piccalilli and chutney out for him.

'Have you any wine?' he said. 'It's been a long day.'

'Won't Sharon wonder where you are?' I said.

'She's at her sister's house again. I don't know what she does over there.'

Probably make Tiktoks and giggle, but he'd never understand that. I poured us each a glass of red wine.

'Let's eat before it gets cold.'

The food filled a large part of the black hole left by Joy's revelation about the woman seen on the pier. As the calories infiltrated my bloodstream, I could feel my brain engage. George glanced at me.

'Feeling better?' he said. 'I noticed you were hangry.'

'Did you?'

I tried not to show my surprise. It wasn't like him to take my moods into account or to use millennial slang.

'Shall we go to the sitting room?' he said. 'I'll tell you what's happening.'

We sat on the sofa sipping our wines. It was hard not to enjoy the familiarity of it. Harry's apparent desertion had hurt my feelings. The memory of Joy's advice prodded me in the ribs, but I ignored it. There was a time to clear the air with George, and this did not strike me as propitious. I needed to find out the latest from the station while George was receptive.

'Is Flo back yet?' I said. 'We miss her at Fat Fighters.'

The corner of his mouth crinkled upwards.

'Fishing, Ms Bowe? It's not like you to be so circumspect.'

'How can I help you if you won't help me? I need to know how David died.'

'Don't we all? Someone pushed him into the bulkhead after Roz removed the cigarettes. What I don't get is who else would do that except Ed. He knew he could throw the body overboard without anyone noticing. Why would anyone else stuff the body in there? Who else knew David would be on board?'

'Maybe they killed him by mistake?'

'Well, at least Flo can tell us that tomorrow.'

'Tomorrow?'

'She's back at last.'

'Thank goodness,' I said. 'It will be great to narrow down the pool of suspects.'

'Is there anything else I should know?'

The way he asked caused me to blush.

'I think I'm menopausal,' I said. 'This wine is giving me a hot flush.'

'You always were a terrible liar. I know you spoke to Joy today. We have acquired CCTV feed from a street near the harbour on the night of the murder. A woman can be seen running away from there on the feed not long before the boat leaves the pier. She has a big mop of light-coloured curly hair and she's wearing a floaty dress. She has been identified as Roz Murray. I'm afraid it puts her firmly in the spotlight for David's murder. Maybe Ed as well. They could have acted together. Maybe Roz lured David to the boat.'

'But she took the cigarettes out before David left the Shanty.'

'The CCTV shows her returning along the street to the harbour at about ten fifty.'

'Oh. Can I see it?'

'No. It's police evidence now. It's her, Tan. I saw the footage myself. Maybe she had a fight with David, and Ed helped her put the body in the bulkhead.'

'But Roz wouldn't kill someone. I know her.'

'Maybe not as well as you think.'

'What about David's phone? Does that have messages or evidence about his last evening?'

'We don't have his phone. Whoever killed him removed it. By the way, do you know anything about his background? I'd like to contact his relatives, but we're coming up blank on his past.'

'I talked to one of the stakeholders the other day, Frank Burgess, who owns a dredging business in Shoreham. He told me David had secrets and made insinuations about his dodgy past.'

George rolled his eyes and sighed.

'I won't ask you why you were talking to him, but you should have told me this before. As long as you give me any information you get regarding the case as soon as possible, I'll let it go.'

'Okay, I promise. By the way, it might be worth talking to Lexi again. She worked with him for ten years.'

'I'll get her in to interview. She wasn't exactly forthcoming last time. Didn't she tell me David was an orphan? We are trying to piece together a profile of him so we can make a complete list of suspects. There may be someone in his past who resurfaced, but we can't find any references to him in the databases. It's almost like he's a ghost.'

It occurred to me that Mouse would love to ferret in the archives for information on David. He had a genuine talent for digging up information most people couldn't retrieve. George never considered Andy (as he called him) had any talents besides hot wiring cars and bringing shame on his head. Resentment at George's refusal to take any of his son's choices into account bubbled in my chest. I stood up, almost knocking over the half-full wine glasses on the table.

'You should go home. I've got another long day tomorrow.'

'Really? I haven't finished my wine.'

'You shouldn't drink any more. Didn't you come in your car?'

Out of the corner of my eye, I spotted Hades pawing at the cat flap. I pulled George up by the hand. He groaned and patted his stomach.

'I don't suppose I can sleep on the couch,' he said.

'I hope you're joking.'

He guffawed.

'Of course.'

'Goodnight George.'

He lunged towards me, but I skipped to one side and held the door open. I'm not sure how I felt, apart from confused. He shook his head and put on his jacket, doing up the buttons with great deliberation. I gave him a gentle push, and he stumbled out into the dark.

'Night, Tan.'

I shut him out and went to let Hades in the back entrance. He bounded past me and into his basket. Ungrateful brat. I heard a key in the door and Mouse came in, looking dishevelled and sweaty.

'Why was George here again?' he said. 'Is he bothering you?'

'No, he's just confused. I'm not sure the whole Sharon thing is as easy as he imagined it would be. And David's case is not straightforward either.'

'He can't be very bright if he prefers her to you. No wonder he can't solve the case.'

I beamed.

'Did you have a good time with Amanda?'

'Pretty amazing. She's a brilliant dancer.'

'I'm so happy you're having fun together. Would you like a cup of hot chocolate to take to bed?'

'Yes, please.'

Chapter 18

The police arrested Roz before I got the chance to speak to her again. The news of her arrest spread like wildfire around Seacastle once Grace Wong found out about it. She rivalled Roz in her ability to spread gossip. She turned up breathless at the Second Home, desperate to be the first to tell me. I had never seen her run before and had the urge to laugh as I watched her knock-kneed progress along the high street. I opened the door for her and she bent double, fighting for breath as I waited patiently for her to recover.

'Good morning,' I said. 'Why the great hurry? Have you repented and decided to buy my shoal of taxidermy fish?'

She shuddered.

'No way. You're stuck with them. I've just heard some important news, and I wanted to tell you before someone else did.'

She didn't smile, so I realised it couldn't be the latest gossip about her over-sexed neighbours' activities. I patted her arm.

'Go on then. Spill the beans.'

'Max went to the police station to report a shoplifter for stealing from our shop, and he saw them taking Roz in for questioning.'

'Roz? Are you sure? But how does he know she's at the station?'

'That girl at the desk. You know. Whatsername.'

'Sally.'

'That's her. She told him they found Roz on the CCTV from the harbour on the night of the murder.'

'But they already knew she –'

I stopped myself. Grace did not need to know about the cigarettes.

'They already knew what?'

'Nothing. I don't understand what's going on. First Ed and now Roz. This is terrible,' I said, and meant it.

'I'm sorry. It must be a shock for you.'

'It is. But I'm not worried. There's simply no way Ed or Roz murdered anybody.'

'I hope you're right. Roz can be rather volatile.'

As if I needed reminding. Grace refused a hot beverage, but she carried off a rather splendid embroidered fire screen with her. She always had her business head on, and I made a nice profit, so we were both content.

I paid a visit to the police station to ask if I could see Roz, but Sally Wright shook her head at me.

'Roz is not allowed visitors until the team has finished questioning her. I'm afraid they have sent her to HMP Bronzefield until she can answer the charges in court.'

'HMP Bronzefield?'

'It's a women's prison in Surrey, about an hour from here. Our station doesn't have room to keep female prisoners for long, as we only have a few holding cells and limited facilities. Obviously, Roz can't share a cell with a man, so they had decided she would be safer at the prison.'

'Can I bring her something?'

'They won't let her take anything to the prison with her. But you can visit her any time you like as she's on remand and not sentenced.'

'How do I organise that?'

'Roz needs to book it on the internal system and send you a time. It will take a few days, though. She has to finish her induction and get settled in.'

'Thank you. Can you tell her I came, please? And to book a visit for me anytime. I'll drop everything.'

'Of course. Don't worry. It's a modern prison and quite comfortable. She'll be fine.'

Her unexpected kindness made me teary-eyed and I couldn't answer because of the lump in my throat. I muttered a farewell and walked back to the office. I spent the day fretting, as I couldn't decide which was worse. Roz being incarcerated or Ghita finding out about it. I suspected the shock might reduce Ghita's ire, but I couldn't be sure.

Lexi and Amanda were not as shocked as me about Roz being arrested, being convinced Roz and David had a fling.

'Roz is a hothead,' said Lexi. 'Something went wrong. Maybe he made a pass at her and she shoved him too hard.'

'He wouldn't take no as an answer,' said Amanda, crossing her arms over her breasts in a protective gesture. 'He believed in his droit de seigneur.'

'Don't exaggerate,' said Lexi.

'I'm not exaggerating,' said Amanda, and I caught her eye. A glazed look came down like a shutter. I needed to ask her some questions, but not when her defences were up.

'Have either of you seen David's phone?' I said.

'Why do you ask?' said Lexi.

'The police need to review the contents.'

'I haven't seen his phone, but he had it on the night of the murder,' said Amanda. 'I remember him checking his texts.'

It occurred to me that her story had changed. I remembered her telling me she hadn't seen him on the night of the murder, but this slip of the tongue told me she had. I had not considered the fact Amanda might have been the last person to see David. She definitely had a crush on him. Had he given her the brush off when he brought her the memory cards? She seemed to have fun with Mouse, but I didn't know how she really felt about him. I decided to catch her alone as soon as I could. I wondered if I should alert Lexi to George's wish to interview her again and decided it was none of my business.

Before I could think of an excuse to get Amanda on her own, my cell phone pinged at me. Flo! My spirits rose as I scanned her text. George has given her permission to tell me the results of the autopsy on condition I didn't tell anyone before the newspapers published the information. I needed some normality after the depressing news about Roz. I texted Flo back, inviting her to the Grotty Hovel for supper. On my way home, I bought some pork chops and a jar of applesauce. Flo loved pork in all its manifestations, and I imagined she had severe cravings after being in Egypt for a few weeks. I put the chops in the oven and made some mashed potato with plenty of butter and pepper. I left a bottle of cider in the freezer, praying I remembered to take it out before it froze. The doorbell rang and a tanned, slimmed-down version of my friend stood with her arms out. I accepted a fragrant hug.

'Wow! You look fabulous,' I said. 'Egypt agrees with you.'

'Actually, it didn't. I had diarrhoea for three weeks after I ate salad in a restaurant. But I lost a stone in weight, so there's a silver lining to every cloud.'

She grinned and took in a deep breath.

'I could eat the air in here. Is that pork I smell?'

'Pork chops. I hope you're hungry.'

'I could eat a whole pig.'

'Excellent.'

Soon we were seated at the table with large tankards of cider and plates heaving with delicious food. Mouse had yet again disappeared with Amanda after work so we could broach confidential subjects without fear of being overheard. Flo mopped up the last of the gravy from her plate and dropped a bit of gristle on the floor for Hades. He gobbled it up and sat beside her chair, ever hopeful of a second piece. She patted him on the head.

'You're out of luck, kid.'

He arched his back and let her stroke him. I almost threw my napkin at him. Cheeky maggot! He still wouldn't come near me.

'Is everything okay down at the station?' I said.

Flo didn't answer right away. Her eyes twinkled as she enjoyed my discomfort. I put on my pleading face.

'Don't be mean. I know George told you that you could tell me.'

'He was murdered,' she said. 'Definitely.'

'How do you know?'

'Because he had a bullet wound. The others didn't see it because the blood from his head wound had soaked his clothes. I noticed it when I stripped the body.'

'Someone shot him? What sort of gun?'

'That's the weird thing. The bullet is ancient .380 calibre issued in the 1950s. The techies think it might have been shot from an Enfield no. 2 Revolver. Army issue. They've been out of service for decades.'

'Did you find the bullet?'

'It had pierced his heart and lodged in his spine. He probably died instantly.'

'That's horrible. Have they contacted his relatives yet?'

'I don't think so. Wasn't he an orphan?'

'He might have an uncle or aunt or someone else.'

After Flo had left, I wrote some notes on the case and I realised that Emily, Frank Burgess's secretary might have the information we needed to help us trace David's past. I suspected she would tell Harry anything he wanted to know to impress him. The thought of her cosying up to him at the historical talk about pill boxes had already freaked me out, but if he could find out something vital about David, I could swallow my objection to their date. Maybe if I showed him, I could be grown up about it, he would forgive my unnecessary jealousy. I dialled his number.

'Hallo mate. Why so late? Have you got a proposition for me?'

'Not the sort you're thinking. But I would like you to do me a favour. Are you still going to that pill box talk with Emily?'

'I am. Why?'

'Can you find out why Frank Burgess told me David was a fraud? He insinuated David got what he deserved.'

'You didn't tell me that. It could be really important.'

'I'm sorry. The Emily thing threw me off.'

'The Emily thing?'

I could hear him laughing and my heart leapt.

'You silly old moo. Are you jealous?'

'Um, maybe.'

'Honestly, I leave you alone for five minutes and all hell breaks loose. We're partners, aren't we?'

'I suppose so.'

'Don't suppose anything. We've been through a lot together. You're a member of my platoon now. I won't let you down. And I certainly won't abandon you for another while we're still healing our war wounds. Emily is collateral damage. She's not important.'

'That's a little mean.'

'You know what I'm trying to say. Hang in there. I'll find out what's going on with Frank and David.'

After I hung up the phone, I felt like an idiot. I don't know why I doubted Harry. My self-confidence took a beating when I succumbed to depression. I had always thought of myself as strong, both in terms of body and mind. Depression made me admit I needed help and taught me humility. I think that's why I didn't blame George for leaving me. He couldn't cope with it either. We had often rolled our eyes in unison when we heard people talking about it. I had inherited my mother's attitude to depression, and thought I should just pull up my socks. Unfortunately, the big D had other ideas, and soon pulling them on was more than I could manage some days.

Now I had recovered my normal life, but my confidence had been shaken to the core. Investigating the death of my friend Mel Conrad had given me back my zest for life, and now I had the chance to use my investigative skills again, I would not turn down the chance to exonerate my friends. Harry had the annoying habit of always being right. I had allowed myself to doubt him, but it wouldn't happen again. Roz and Ed needed us to work as a team, and there was no way I'd give up on them, either. I had to get Roz out of Bronzefield as soon as I could. We needed to investigate David's background and find out why someone hated him enough to kill him.

Chapter 19

Mouse couldn't have been happier when I asked him to use his hacking skills to find out about David de Frontenac's murky past. He set himself up in the window seat of the café, barricaded off from visitors by a couple of sturdy kitchen chairs. He had become a fixture in the Vintage, as the café was called. Many people with zero interest in vintage or antique goods made a detour to the cheap end of the high street, just to have a coffee and make eyes at Mouse. His regency good looks appealed to the Mills and Boon crowd and he flirted with everybody, regardless of age. He enjoyed the attention and always had time for the shy or lonely. I felt privileged to be his sort-of stepmother.

Our lunchtime regulars came and went that day, but Mouse never left his seat in the window. I tried my best to be welcoming and social, but some raised eyebrows made it clear the clientele considered me a poor substitute. I'm better at sarcastic banter than small talk, and it shows. Even a large angry herring gull tapping the window with its beak and demanding food failed to distract Mouse from his search. The clouds scudded past on a fresh breeze and I shut the windows to prevent the napkins blowing off the tables. As I passed by, I gave him an absentminded kiss on the top of his head. How could I be unhappy with such riches?

Amanda made Mouse a sandwich and a cup of tea, and they sat together chatting and scrolling through their phones. I noticed Mouse shut his laptop when she came over to him. It told me he didn't want her to know about his search, which I found interesting. Amanda had showed signs of a crush on David, but I thought her interest in Mouse had cancelled it out. Perhaps they had a past? I hoped Mouse would not discover things he would find distressing. His search was bound to turn up some of David's secrets, good or bad. I hadn't told Lexi about our continuing interest in David's murder. She did not seem surprised to learn he had been murdered, and she didn't seem that interested in finding out who did it either.

Instead, she had gone back to her job of convincing the stakeholders to vote for the sanctuary. Since he had been murdered, Lexi had leaned on them to create it as his legacy, an argument which seemed to work better than saving the environment. David's murder had generated a mountain of free publicity for the sanctuary which she intended to milk.

'This is our fifteen minutes of fame,' she said. 'I can drum up hundreds of projects for the consultancy on the back of it.'

She posed for photographs and endured many carbon-copy interviews, sounding devastated and determined to carry on David's legacy in all of them. Her telephone never stopped ringing. Amanda fielded the calls and emailed the consultancy bank details to donors and took on more responsibility in the company. Lexi's approval grew as her appreciation of what Amanda could do increased.

My phone rang, startling me out of my reverie. I strained to hear the voice on the line.

'Tanya, is that you? It's me, Roz.'

Her voice sounded insubstantial and fearful like she had called me while hiding in a cupboard.

'It's me. Where are you?'

'They've put me in a prison. I, I…'

She wailed, a sound that threatened to tear my heart in two.

'It's to keep you safe,' I said. 'Be brave and don't worry. I'm allowed to visit you as often as you like.'

I heard her gulping and sniffing. She stopped crying and took a deep breath.

'They told me I can have visitors any time during visiting hours. I just need to book a time for you. It may take a few days, though.'

'Book it as soon as you can. I'm working on solving this, but I need you to tell me what really happened that night.'

'But I already told you.'

'You must tell me everything. Including the bit you missed out. It's important.'

Roz didn't answer for so long, I thought we'd been cut off.

'I'll text the time of the visit as soon as I get one,' she said, finally.

'Chin up. We love you.'

Mouse raised his eyebrows in question at me as I approached him in the café.

'Who died?' he said.

'They've taken Roz to Bronzefield. It's a prison—'

'I know what it is,' he said, cutting me off, and then shrugged. 'I'm sorry. What can I do?'

I realised his delinquent past might be responsible for that knowledge and didn't react to his rudeness.

'I don't think there's much you can do for now. Have you found out anything about David?'

'I know one thing. He didn't exist eleven years ago. At least there is no trace of anyone with his name anywhere. There's a hotel in Paris and a famous one in Toronto called Chateau Frontenac, but I can't find any family with that name who might be related to him. David is a phantom.'

'Lexi told George she had known David most of her life and worked with him for ten years.'

'She might know more about David than she's letting on. I think you should ask her.'

'I intend to, but I'm waiting for Harry to get some answers from Emily first.'

Mouse gazed at me for a few seconds. I could feel my face reddening under his scrutiny.

'Are you okay with him seeing Emily? I mean, do you, um…'

'Not really. But Roz is my dear friend, and I'd do anything for her. I have to trust Harry. He says I'm not to worry, and that's good enough for me.'

He hadn't finished with me. His eyebrows came together and I could almost hear his mind whirring.

'Does Harry know about George?'

'There's nothing to know.'

'But he keeps coming to our house. Why don't you tell him to go away?'

'It's complicated. I don't know how to explain it to you. I want him to stay away, but I also want him to turn up. He divorced me, not the other way around. I thought we were happy.'

'What about Sharon?'

'She stole George from me. I don't feel too bad about borrowing him back.'

Mouse sighed.

'I don't like him coming to the house,' he said.

'I know. I'll talk to him. It's something I've been avoiding. Somehow, our relationship hasn't quite finished yet, and I'm not sure if I want to kill it stone dead. Can you understand that?'

He didn't answer. I could imagine how Mouse felt about George. He represented a threat to our little household. If George and I got back together Mouse couldn't see himself fitting into the new scenario. Mouse was right. I had to decide between them, or I was playing with fire. I hadn't told Harry about George's visits to the Grotty Hovel, because I had kidded myself that I didn't need to. After all, there was nothing going on. But was I lying to myself too?

Chapter 20

Harry called in to the shop the next morning, as bright and breezy as a Seacastle day. He gave me a long hug, which would keep me warm for ages.

'Hello mate. Get the kettle on. I'm gasping for a cuppa.'

'What's the magic word?'

'Cake?'

I resisted the temptation to hug him again.

'Come on. I think there's a slice of coffee and walnut left.'

'My favourite.'

We went upstairs and I couldn't help remembering I hadn't yet paid him for the taxidermy fish who stared goggle eyed and accusing at me.

'Did you enjoy the lecture?' I said, without turning around, as I made him a big mug of strong tea. He didn't answer until I brought the tea over.

'I found it fascinating,' he said, and winked.

'Just the lecture?'

'Only the lecture. Scout's honour.'

I grinned.

'Could you get anything out of Emily?'

He guffawed.

'Not that,' I said. 'Behave.'

'Sorry, I couldn't resist it. She clammed up when I asked questions and claimed to have no idea what Burgess meant.'

'That's annoying.'

'However.'

'However, what?'

'She told me Burgess had written Hull beside David's name on a notepad he had used to take notes during the meeting at the Vintage. It made little sense to her, but then she remembered Burgess's daughter went to University in Hull.'

'Hull?' said Mouse. 'He didn't have the right accent.'

'How weird. Do you think Burgess knew him from there? David's accent made me think public school, with possibly upper-class origins,' I said.

'Let me have a look,' said Mouse.

He tapped away at the keyboard, and clicked on page links, nodding his head and biting his bottom lip in concentration. I shut my eyes and tried to hear David's voice in my head. I could picture his handsome face with ease, but his voice had already faded.

'Hang on,' said Mouse. 'I think I've got something.'

We waited with bated breath while he scanned the page. Suddenly, his eyes lit up.

'There's an Environmental Sciences degree course at Hull University. What year do you think David did his degree?'

'He must have been about forty, although he appeared to be in his early thirties. Lexi said they grew up together, so you can ask her when she turns up. Why don't you check from 1995 to 2010?' I said.

'I can hack into student records and look at the photographs for Environmental Sciences for those years. It will take me a while to get it, though.'

'Well, I can't hang around long. I've got a delivery,' said Harry.

'And I 've got to visit Roz,' I said.

'I can't believe she's in the nick. I never imagined our Roz doing bird,' said Harry.

'She's not. Being on remand is not the same as being sentenced,' said Mouse.

'Whoa, I was only joking. Don't throw a wobbly on me,' said Harry.

'She'll be out soon,' I said. 'The police have nothing on her.'

'Except the CCTV and the visit to the boat,' said Harry. 'Are you sure she's innocent?'

'I'm sure she's hiding something, but it's not murder,' I said. 'I'll try to find out today.'

Mouse had already put his head down again, so I left with Harry as Lexi and Amanda arrived. He made for his van and I headed for the Mini. I placed my phone on the dashboard and switched on the GPS. Mouse had programmed in the prison's address and showed me how to get it on screen. I congratulated myself on my techie abilities. It wasn't so long before that I couldn't send a text message. I drove north to Leatherhead and then got on the M25. The traffic flowed without delays and soon I turned off the A30 towards Ashford before taking the turning to the prison. As I drove up to the prison car park, I took in its immense size. It looked modern and clean, but the high fences gave its purpose away.

I found the idea of visiting a prison intimidating, but the visitors' centre had clear signposting, which reduced my stress levels a little. After having my credentials checked against the visitor list, they directed me to the visits hall where I handed in my phone and keys. I kept some coins for the coffee machine, but I had to leave everything else behind. I also had to undergo a scan and a rub down search which I found intrusive in the extreme. The airlock doors opened into the visiting hall and I spotted Roz in a corner by her mop of curly hair. I hardly recognised her. Her face looked grey with anxiety. I waved at her and she tried to smile. I pointed at the coffee machine and she nodded. The coffee smelt like a pair of Mouse's dirty socks, but I managed not to grimace as I brought the cups over to our table. She took my hand and gripped it tight.

'Honestly. I know you like to lock yourself away sometimes, but aren't you overdoing it?' I said.

A ghost of a smile crept onto her face.

'This isn't the holiday I had planned. But I have my own room and all my meals are prepared for me.'

'Luxury. I don't know why you are complaining.'

Colour crept back to her cheeks.

'I'm so glad you're here. I thought I might go mad. It's so weird in here. Like boarding school, but stricter.'

'You won't be in here long if I can help it. Are you going to tell me the truth about what happened that night or not?'

'It's not what you want to hear.'

'Tell me anyway. What happened after you put the cigarettes in the beach hut?'

Time stood still for a moment as she composed herself. I looked around at the over-bright graphics on the walls of the visiting hall. Laughing cartoons disporting themselves without a care in the world. The sound of murmured conversations around us got drowned out by the screams of children playing around their mothers. I wondered how you explained to a child that their mother had to stay in prison and couldn't come home with them. Roz cleared her throat and stared into the distance as if visualising that night.

'I planned to go home after I stored the cigarettes, but David turned up at the beach hut. He'd seen me from the road when he'd been walking to Ed's boat. His breath smelled of beer and he didn't seem steady on his feet.'

'Joy told me he'd been in the Shanty.'

'That explains it. Anyway, he tried to persuade me to go on the boat with him and Ed, but I didn't want to. I went to push past him, but he grabbed me and stopped me from leaving. He shoved me up against the hut. I don't know if he meant to be so rough, but he scared me. And then he started pawing me and kissing me. I...'

Her head dropped into her hands, and she ran her fingers through her hair. When she spoke again, I had to lean right in to hear her.

'I pushed him hard, and he fell backwards over a lobster pot and hit his head. I waited for him to move, but he stayed down. Then Ed appeared on his way to the boat. He had also spotted me and came over to find out what I was doing. He noticed David lying there. I didn't tell him what had happened exactly, only that David had been drunk and had fallen over the lobster pot. Ed insisted I go home. He said he would deal with it. I assumed he would call an ambulance or something. I was so shocked that I just went home to bed. Only Ed knows what happened next.'

Her hands were shaking when I reached out for them. She looked into my eyes.

'I must have killed him. Ed is covering for me. That's the only explanation. But I won't let him.'

'I can understand that, but why did you go back to the boat later on that night?'

She lifted her head and her brow furrowed.

'I didn't. I went home. Ed told me to go to bed and stay there. So I did.'

'But how did Ed get the body into the boat? There's no way he could have carried him alone.'

'I don't know. Maybe he used a trolley? There's plenty of them down on the pier for moving fish boxes.'

I squeezed her hand.

'I spoke to Flo about the autopsy yesterday. David didn't die from a fall.'

'What? I don't believe you.'

'Seriously. Someone shot him. With an old army pistol.'

Roz turned as white as snow, and I thought she would faint. Two small children chased each other around our table, oblivious to her shock. I tried to shoo them away and shot an appealing look at their mother who totally ignored me. Roz recovered a little and shook her head.

'No,' she said. 'I don't believe you.'

'This is good news. You didn't kill him. You must tell the police the truth. They will have to release you.'

'You understand nothing,' said Roz. 'You've got to go now. I'm tired.'

'But Roz—'

'It's too late,' she said, shaking her head. 'What am I going to do? The police will find the pistol and then they'll know.'

'Know what?'

But she stood up and marched out of the hall.

Chapter 21

I had intended to stay with Roz for a couple of hours, but she did not reappear in the visitors' hall. After an hour, the security guard told me I had run out of time and had to leave. I lingered outside the prison and watched people come and go, wondering what it would be like to be incarcerated for years in such a place. A heavy drizzle spotted my jacket, and I retreated inside the Mini. Then my mobile phone pinged as a text arrived from Flo. She told me she would drop by the shop after work with important news about the case.

I shook myself back to the present and started the engine. Roz and Ed needed me. Moping in a car park would help no one. I put on a rock and roll mix Harry had made for me and turned the volume up high. Despite some of my favourite tracks booming out from the speakers, I drove home from the prison with a heavy heart. Roz would never tell the police what happened that night, because she thought Ed had shot David after she had left. I found it impossible to believe that of Ed. He had a hot temper, but he wouldn't shoot a man in cold blood. As far as I could make out, Roz hadn't actually told him about the assault. What reason would Ed have to shoot him? I had to find Ed and persuade him to tell me the truth before Roz ended up in the magistrate's court.

The trip to Seacastle took me nearly an hour and a half after I hit traffic on the M25. I ate half a large bar of Cadbury's Fruit and Nut out of anxiety and misery. Then I got soaked running to Second Home after I parked the car. Mouse took one look at me when I got back to the shop and made me a milky coffee with two teaspoons of sugar. I took the towel from the toilet and mopped ineffectually at my wet clothes. Mouse sat opposite me and frowned at my sodden state.

'Did you swim back?' he said.

'Hilarious. Look outside, nerdy boy. An Ark just floated down High Street.'

He ignored my joke.

'How was it?' he said.

'Bleak and weird.'

'And Roz?'

I tried to answer, but my bottom lip trembled and hot tears crawled down my cheeks. Mouse put his arm around my shoulders and passed me napkins while I cried.

'It's such a mess,' I said, eventually. 'Roz thinks Ed did it and Ed thinks Roz did it. They're both willing to go to jail for each other. How can it get any worse?'

But it did. Flo arrived not long after me, her normally neat bun bedraggled with long strands of greying hair hanging down her back. I ushered her upstairs where only Mouse remained. Amanda and Lexi had gone to some junket to raise money for the consultancy and give interviews on David's untimely demise. I wondered how much either of them knew about his violent streak. Roz couldn't be the only woman he attempted to assault. Flo stood in front of a Victorian mirror and redid her bun.

'I thought you should know,' she said without looking at me. 'Ed turned himself into the police station today. He also handed in a World War II Enfield revolver and some bullets wrapped in a piece of shammy leather. His prints were all over the gun. He's been arrested again.'

'Are they going to let Roz go?'

'I shouldn't imagine so. George thinks they conspired to murder him together. They would have got away with it if Len hadn't put the cigarettes behind the bulkhead.'

'Do you believe that?' I said.

I must have sounded incredulous. She turned to look at me.

'It's not a question of belief. We follow the evidence, and at present it suggests they are guilty. We already had David's body on Ed's boat, and Roz on the CCTV feed an hour after she said she went home. Now we have the murder weapon.'

'Have you tested it already?'

Flo shook her head.

'No, but it has Ed's fingerprints all over it.'

'He did that on purpose,' I said. 'What murderer leaves their prints all over the murder weapon? He's trying to incriminate himself.'

'He also shoved a body in the bulkhead and set out to sea with it. If he's innocent, why didn't he call the police?' said Flo.

I couldn't answer that. How had the body got from the beach huts to the boat? And if it was Ed who moved it, how did it get a bullet in it without him knowing?

'I don't know. All I can be sure of is that they're covering for each other, but we're missing a piece of the puzzle. Someone else must be involved.'

'But there's no evidence of anyone else being on the boat.'

'There's no CCTV on the pier. Maybe someone else shot David on Ed's boat.'

'Why didn't he shoot Ed too? We've got to face facts. It's looking bad for Roz and Ed.'

I shrugged.

'I can't accept they're guilty. There's something missing here.'

'And if the bullets match Ed's weapon?'

I didn't know how to answer that.

'Will you let me know?'

'Not officially. But yes, I will,' said Flo.

'Do you want to get something to eat?'

'No, I've got to go home. I want to watch the last episode of some Swedish crime noir I've been watching.'

'What's it called?' I said.

'Something unpronounceable.' Flo hugged me. 'I'll be in touch,' she said.

I stood at the top of the stairs watching her leave and I stayed there for ages, the cogs in my brain turning with no result. A feeling of panic and claustrophobia almost overwhelmed me. Had I been wrong all along? Were Roz and Ed capable of murder? I felt faint, and I grabbed the bannister.

'Are you okay?' said Mouse.

'No, I'm not. I'm going for a walk down to the pier. If I don't get some fresh air, I may suffocate.'

I pulled on my leather jacket and zipped it up against the cool breeze whistling down the high street. I put my head down and strode into it, finding solace in the effort. My hair streamed behind me as I emerged from the side streets into the harbour. I made for the bench sheltered from the wind by the harbour wall and sat down. An icy drizzle swept in sideways, crept over the top of the wall and down my neck. I regretted my decision to clear my head in the rain. I went to leave when someone sat down beside me. I recognised him as Pat Grady from the coastguard office. He had on a bright yellow raincoat which covered him from head to foot, but his ratty face poked out of the hood. He sniffed the air, looking even more rodent like, and lit a cigarette.

'What you doing out here in the rain, Miss,' he said, blowing out some toxic smelling smoke. 'Hey, didn't you come into my office the other day with Roz Murray?'

'I did. There's been a lot of water under the bridge since then.'

'So they tell me. It weren't her, you know.'

He shook his head and took another drag on his cigarette. I wondered if he would give me one. The temptation to smoke had never been stronger. I felt like I had been hit with one disaster after another. I nodded.

'I didn't think it was. But it doesn't look good. The evidence points at both of them.'

'Them thar police should've listened to me, though. I know things.'

He leaned forward with his elbows on his knees and a large drop of water slid down his nose and splashed onto the pier. Since he didn't elaborate, I risked a question.

'Can you tell me what you know? I'll believe you.'

He wrinkled up his face and peered into mine as if searching for a trick. I kept my expression neutral and waited.

'I tried to tell Roz when she came that time, you know? But she never paid me no mind.'

'I bet she'd listen now,' I said, triggering a ratty snigger from Grady.

'Oh, I bet she would.'

'What did you try to tell her?' I said, thinking uncharitable things about blood and stones.

'The second call. I knew it must be important, but no one bothered to take the time to listen.'

I couldn't believe my ears.

'What second call?'

'That same night. About an hour after the first.'

I felt my blood freeze in my veins.

'Who called?'

'Oh, I don't know. Someone with a muffled voice. It sounded like they were talking through a sock.'

'Could you tell if they were male or female?'

'Not really.'

'What did they say?'

'They told me they wanted to report a murder.'

I almost fell off the bench.

'A murder? Did they say anything else?'

'They told me Ed Murray had a body on his boat, and I laughed and told them I already had a call about Ed's boat. I accused them of pranking me.'

'What happened then?'

'They hung up.'

My mind reeled with a flood of possibilities related to this new information. And then I thought of something else.

'Was there anything odd about the calls, apart from the content?'

'Oh, yes. Definitely.'

'And what was that?'

'Both calls were made from an old-fashioned phone box. I could hear the pips before the coins were inserted.'

My mind whirled as I tried to take this in. It occurred to me that Grady might be a regular on this bench at night. Could he have seen something?

'I guess you're not allowed to smoke in the office,' I said. 'Seeing as you're out here in the rain.'

'I like to take my break on the bench. It clears my head to have five minutes of fresh air.'

Hardly fresh with those stinky cigarettes!

'And did you see anyone heading for the boat on the night of the murder?'

'Oh, yes. I already told the police. I saw Ed Murray walking to the boat over there about ten-thirty.'

'You must have great eyesight. How could you tell it was him?'

'He had one of those fisherman's hoodies on, with the big anchor on the back.'

'Did you see anyone else?'

'No, I went back into the office and finished my shift. That's when I got the second call.'

As I watched him go, I wondered who on earth had made the second call. Knowing the sex of the caller would help, but they had to be at least thirty if they had used the call box.

Chapter 22

I sat in stunned silence for ages after Pat Grady left to go back to his office, digesting this new piece of information. I would have to convey it to George as soon as I could. I wasn't sure how it affected Roz and Ed, but it seemed extraordinary that someone else had known about David's death. Could it be the murderer? Someone touched my arm, and I jumped in fright. I thought Pat Grady had returned, but Mouse stood there in the yellow light, holding an umbrella over me.

'We should go home,' he said.

'You'll never guess what just happened.'

'On a bench in the rain?'

'I had a visit from the coastguard.'

'Is that code for some female bodily function about which I am in total ignorance?'

I roared with laughter.

'No. It's case-breaking news. I'll tell you about it in the car. By the way, did you find out anything about David yet?'

'I'm still working on it. You had some customers today, and I had little chance to hack the archives.'

'Did anyone buy a taxidermy fish?'

'Don't be silly. I didn't say we experienced a miracle.'

'Let's go home. Shall we stop for Chinese?'

'Do I need to answer that?'

I left Mouse in the car scrolling on his phone while I popped into the takeaway near the harbour. I already knew our order by heart, and when the owner saw me enter, he smiled.

'Same as usual?' he said.

'Yes please, Mr Chen.'

'You sit. Five minutes, maybe ten, okay?'

'Great. Thanks.'

I perched on the plastic covered bench to the side of the takeaway and looked around. Tattered red Chinese lanterns hung over the four Formica tables squashed into the small space reserved for customers eating in. The tables all had red-checked PVC-coated covers and wooden benches on either side. Bottles of soy and hoisin sauce with drip marks running down their labels sat on lace mats. The wall paper showed tall multi-floored pagodas beside flat rivers with sampans and junks manned by people with outsized bamboo hats.

My eyes strayed upwards as I heard a mechanical whirring and I spotted a camera in the corner of the ceiling with its red light blinking. I stared up into the lens for a few seconds lost in a reverie, and then it hit me. The police claimed to have Roz on CCTV and George had told me he couldn't let me see it. But what if I found another copy of the feed? Goose, Mouse's friend who put the sockets in the upstairs office had offered to provide CCTV for the shop. I wondered if he had friends who knew from where the police had got their pictures of Roz. Maybe we could exonerate her after all.

I stood up and shifted my weight from foot to foot in impatience. When Mr Chen arrived, he laughed at me.

'You starving,' he said. 'You not want wait.'

I grinned and took the bag.

'Thank you.' I said. 'You're right. I can't.'

I left the restaurant and got back into the Mini, plonking the bag of food on Mouse's lap. He yelped as the steam from the hot rice penetrated his cargo trousers. Then he saw my expression.

'Did Mr Chen give you some rice wine? You look funny,' he said.

'We're back in business.'

'What are you talking about?'

'CCTV.'

'Okay, you lost me. Weren't we going to wait for the tests on Ed's gun?'

'I bet you a million pounds it hasn't been used in anger for nearly a century.'

'So?'

'Can you call Goose for me?'

'Of course. What shall I tell him? Do you want him to install CCTV in Second Home?'

'Ask him if he wants to share our Chinese.'

'You haven't told me what happened on the bench yet.'

I smiled like the cat who got the cream.

'Pat Grady from the coastguard came over to sit with me on his fag break. And it turns out there were two calls about Ed's boat that night.'

'Two calls? Holy shit. That's big. No, scratch that. It's massive.'

'I know. Len made the first call to the coastguard and mentioned contraband on Ed's boat. But the second caller told Pat there was a body behind the bulkhead.'

'Does he know who the caller was?'

'No. They rang off when he asked them why they were calling twice. And they were speaking through a sock or some piece of material to muffle the sound.'

Mouse sat back with his mouth open. I started the car and headed for home, my head spinning with hunger. I couldn't take in the new information without food.

'Don't just sit there,' I said. 'Call Goose. I want him to track down a copy of the CCTV with Roz on it. We need a timeline for the feed and an identification of the person caught on it. Roz told me she went to bed just after ten o'clock and that doesn't fit events at all.'

Mouse scrolled through his phone and found Goose's number.

'I presume this is all confidential,' he said. 'About the phone call?'

'I'll tell your father tomorrow. There's no point calling him today. The investigating team will have gone home for the night.'

'Do you think the murderer made the second call?'

'Maybe. And they may have used the same call box, so George already has their fingerprints.'

Mouse tried to hug me.

'Oi, hands off the driver. Ring Goose. We're on a roll.'

Chapter 23

I woke up the next morning with a foul hangover. I had been so excited about my idea of getting a copy of the incriminating CCTV recording that I had allowed Mouse and Goose to persuade me to drink vodka shots with them. My poor head felt as if I had placed it in a vice and tightened the screws. To make things worse, Hades had placed the bloody remains of a vole on the bathroom floor and I almost trod on it. Bile rose in my throat as I picked it up with fingers covered in a couple of layers of toilet paper and placed it in the bin. I wondered if these gifts were peace offerings, but there was no way of finding out. Hades had actually rubbed himself against my leg in the kitchen while I opened a can of cat food, but jumped away when I lowered a cautious hand to stroke him.

Goose had stumbled out around midnight and crawled into a taxi. I hoped he understood the need for secrecy. He had been ecstatic when we asked him to help acquire the feed. There were only a few CCTV providers in Seacastle and he had worked for all of them. He claimed a kinship with them that would open doors shut to both Mouse and me. I tried to emphasise the need for speed, but by that time we had had so much to drink I wasn't sure he'd remember any instructions. And if he had a headache like mine, I doubted it would be his first priority. I swallowed a couple of Panadol with a glass of milk, followed by an aspirin for good luck. Then I lay down on my bed again after setting the alarm on my phone for an hour later.

The smell of bacon woke me before the alarm, and I was surprised to find my headache had disappeared, or at least had retreated sufficiently for me to feel hunger rather than pain. I staggered down to the kitchen and found Mouse making a large fry up. I opened the back door to let the cooking smells out and Hades sat on the back step, gazing into the brambles. I could see the beginning of buds on the tendrils and imagined the rich harvest of blackberries if I didn't rip the brambles out for another year. I went back into the kitchen and Mouse had laid the table for us. A large pot of strong tea sat beside the ketchup and brown sauce bottles, and I sank my teeth into a bacon butty with a sigh of bliss.

'You're hired,' I said.

Mouse smirked and smothered his butty with brown sauce. I envied his ability to drink like a fish and then wake up with a head as clear as a bell, one I had lost years ago. At least I had given up smoking. That definitely made hangovers less long-lived and ferocious. I gulped down some tea and felt the hot liquid hit my stomach. My look of relief made Mouse laugh.

'Tough morning?' he said.

'My headache is subsiding, and I'm so excited about the CCTV I feel fine.'

He frowned at me and sighed.

'You're presuming we can prove it's not her. But what if it is? What if the gun has been fired recently and the bullets match the one that killed David?' he said. 'Have you thought about that?'

I put down my cup of tea and considered my reply. What if the Murrays had done this horrible thing? What would I do?

'Roz and Ed are my friends. If they killed David, they were forced to. I hope I'll be able to support them. I know they'd support me.'

'What reason could there be?'

'I can't imagine. But they've not been found guilty yet and they're relying on us to help them. That's all that matters right now. Can you please concentrate on searching the university archives this morning? It shouldn't take too long to find David, if he's in there.'

'Do you want me to wash up?'

'You can leave it to soak. I'm keen on getting to the shop. I have some pricing to do.'

'When's your next clearance with Harry?'

'I don't know. He's been busy lately.'

'Have you had a fight?'

'No. We're taking a break. Things are so complicated right now,'

'You know what happened to Ross and Rachel of *Friends* when they were on a break?'

'Not that sort of break.'

But the similarities didn't escape me.

We walked along the promenade in bright sunshine and I could feel my eyes protesting despite wearing my cheap sunglasses to protect them. The high tide had dumped piles of seaweed on the pebbles and the seagulls stalked among the fronds, spearing mussels with their razor-sharp beaks.

'Which do you think is sharper?' said Mouse. 'A herring gull's beak or She-Ra's sword?'

I turned to look at him.

'She-Ra? Even I'm too young to know about She-Ra. Where on earth did you hear about her?'

'I found the Masters of the Universe series online. She's the twin sister of He-Man. She's uber cool. We love She-Ra.'

I tried not to laugh. I found gaming and comic universes incomprehensible, but I preferred Mouse to be obsessed with computers rather than getting drunk or high. Not that I was in a position to lecture after my inadvisable venture the night before. What was I thinking?

We arrived at the shop and Mouse went upstairs to turn on the coffee machine. I gave the wooden furnishings a wipe with some beeswax to keep back the sea of dust that enveloped everything if you turned away for a minute. The telephone rang, and I picked it up.

'Hello, Second Home. Can I help you?'

'It's me, Harry. I've got a clearance today. Can you come with me?'

'What happened to your cell phone?'

'It's a long story. Are you free?'

'Sure. It'll be fun to get out for a few hours. We've had bad news on the murder front and I need a break. Do you want me to make us a flask of tea?'

'Now you're talking. Have you got any cake?'

'I'll send Mouse to get us some chocolate croissants from the French bakery.'

'I'll be there in twenty minutes. I'll text you so you can wait outside when I drive by.'

After sending Mouse sprinting to the bakery, I took my hairbrush out of my handbag and took off my scrunchy. I brushed out my hair and put on some lipstick. I also removed my ratty jumper and put on my black leather jacket. I admired myself in the mirror. Emily had nothing on me. Well, except youth, but nothing else. I made a big pot of tea and decanted it into our largest flask. Mouse came back panting and stuffing a croissant into his mouth as I screwed the second cup on top. I held the flask up to check for leaks.

'Wow. She-Ra had nothing on you,' he said. 'But your sword's not very sharp.'

'I have sharp words which can cut people to ribbons,' I said. 'I don't need a sword.'

The ping of a text told me my impatient steed was arriving, and I gave Mouse a peck on the check and another croissant.

'Don't wait up,' I said, and he winked at me.

'I won't.'

I bounded out to the pavement feeling like a teenager on a day out. I spotted the van as it turned into the high street with Fletcher's Clearance painted on its side. My anticipation of a day's banter and rock music faded as I noticed a second person in the front seat beside Harry. Emily? What on earth was she doing there? Had he collected her first? Or worse, had she stayed the night with him? I almost turned around and went back into the shop. Mouse had come downstairs to wave at Harry, and surprise or shock clouded his features. He shooed me towards the van, mouthing something. Fight? He put up a fist and nodded. With what? How could I compete? She reminded me of a wholesome Disney princess with her perfect teeth, perfect hair and perfect skin. The woman was blander than tofu. I couldn't believe Harry would bring her to a clearance. Did he have any idea how that would make me feel?

The van pulled up beside me, and I avoided looking at Harry. Emily gave me a massive fake smile and my hackles rose. You asked for it, sweet cheeks. I got into the van, trying not to touch her at all. I needn't have worried. She took advantage of the squash to snuggle up to Harry. At least he had the grace to look uncomfortable.

'Oh, hi Amelia,' I said. 'Did you lose your bus pass?'

'My what? Um, it's Emily.'

'You remember Emily, don't you? From Frank Burgess's office,' said Harry, a note of panic entering his voice.

'Oh yes. I had forgotten you worked for that man,' I said, tilting my head on one side. 'We all have our own standards, don't we?'

I thought Harry might implode, but he stared ahead, gripping the steering wheel with white knuckles.

'We're going to drop Emily at the office,' he said.

'That's nice for her,' I said, and patted her leg as if she were a poodle.

The temperature inside the van hit Arctic frost zone, not that Emily seemed to notice. She prattled on and on about some reality show on the television. If I had a cork, I would have used it. After what seemed forever, Harry stopped outside Frank's office in Shoreham. I got out of the van and let Emily exit too. She leaned towards me as if she would kiss me goodbye, but I pretended not to see her. I jumped back into the van and slammed the door. She tapped the window and make cute faces at Harry as we drove off. It was all I could do to give her the slightest of waves. I couldn't risk saying anything to Harry without having a rant at him, and I knew that wouldn't help. Instead, I put on AC-DC at high volume. Instead of enjoying it, I felt my headache coming back, tightening like a band around my head. Harry tolerated one track and then he leaned over and turned down the music.

'I'm sorry about that,' he said. 'She insisted on coming with me in the van to see you. She really likes you.'

I rolled my eyes. Men. Honestly.

'Does she? That's nice. Are you sleeping with her?'

I hadn't meant to blurt it out like that, but my emotions were exploding. He flexed his fingers on the steering wheel and took a deep breath.

'I don't think you're one to talk about sleeping with other people,' he said.

'What? Who told you that?'

'Okay, let's play detective since you enjoy it so much. I'll ask you some questions and you answer them with the truth.'

I should have refused, but I needed to know why he thought that.

'Okay. Shoot.'

'Why was George's car parked outside your house the other morning before work? And while we're on the subject, why was the same car parked outside your house very late a couple of nights ago?'

I stared at him.

'What were you doing there?' I said.

'I wanted to surprise you with a chair I found before you left for work. And the other evening I was in the neighbourhood and I thought we could have a takeaway or something.'

I deflated, all bravado gone, and sighed.

'George is having problems with Sharon. She has put him on a diet and he's starving all the time. He came round one morning, supposedly to talk about the case, but, really, he just wanted feeding. Also, he knows Roz is one of my best friends, and he is doing his best to keep me updated.'

'And the other night?'

'He brought a takeaway with the pretext of talking about the case. And, yes, I think he's being too attentive. Sharon is not the woman he thought he wanted. Mouse told me I should tell you, but I didn't know how. And you haven't been around. Only I realise now that you have.'

Harry rubbed his chin.

'I didn't sleep with Emily,' he said. 'She turned up at my house last night with some information about Frank, which turned out to be useless. I dropped the phone when she tried to grab it from me, and the screen cracked. I left it in for repair on my way to pick you up.'

'She slept in your spare room?'

'I locked my door.'

I laughed.

'So, we're both being stalked?'

'It's hardly surprising. Just look at us.'

I couldn't help smiling.

'I promise not to sleep with George without asking you first.'

'Ditto.'

'Please don't sleep with George. I'd be so jealous.'

'Put the music back on, woman.'

Chapter 24

We pulled up to a semi-detached house in an estate with rows of similar buildings set along roadways, which ended in a turning circle. Most of the front gardens had long been concreted over to form dull grey driveways, but some diehards still had pretty privet hedges and neat lawns. Harry stopped outside number twenty-three, where the lawn had gone to seed and families of sparrows fought in the hedge. The owner sat in her car smoking with the windows shut. She had the orange complexion and swollen lips of a social media influencer. I wondered how she would feel in ten years' time when the tinkering she had done to her looks aged her badly.

She jumped out of the car and I saw she had skinny jeans and a crop top on despite it being about twelve degrees outside. Harry put on his 'I'm completely harmless' grin and stuck out his hand. She took the tips of his fingers and then dropped them as if she might catch something.

'You're the junk people?' she said. 'You're late.'

'I think we agreed to meet at eleven?' said Harry. 'It's ten to now.'

'I've been waiting at least five minutes.'

I hid a smile.

'I'm sorry about that,' said Harry. 'Now, you told me you want me to take all the furniture out for you and scrap it. Is that still the plan?'

'That's right. My father came from Sweden and he has all this weird old stuff. I don't want it at my house. I only have new furniture in my homes.'

'And I'm sure you have exquisite taste,' said Harry, in a soothing tone.

'How much do I have to pay you?' she said, and took a wad of notes out of her back pocket.

'A hundred should cover it,' said Harry.

I smirked.

'Just pull the door to when you leave and put the key through the letterbox,' she said, almost tripping over a small azalea bush which had survived the neglect. She kicked it and frowned. 'You don't know anyone who can concrete this jungle for me, do you? I can't stand plants.'

Harry assured her he could not help, and she got back into her car, lighting another cigarette and scrolling on her phone before she left.

'Did she say Swedish?' I said, crossing my fingers.

'Why? Is that good?'

'It could be.'

It was. After weeks of bad luck, the sun came out for our business. As I walked through the hall door and peered down the corridor into the kitchen, I could see an Alvar Aarto L-leg table and some matching stools with coloured tops. They turned out to be in almost mint condition. The rest of the house yielded several other pieces of unmistakable classic Swedish design, including another Alvar Aarto table with a maple wood top. I pointed the pieces out to Harry, but he didn't seem that impressed.

'If you want them, they're yours,' he said, as he carried them out to the van.

It wasn't until mid-morning I realised I hadn't told Harry or George about the second phone call. I guess I had been so preoccupied with the Emily incident it had totally slipped my mind. I sat out on the wall and called George.

'What do you want now?' he said. 'Is Andy causing trouble? This investigation is stalled and I've got the Super breathing down my neck.'

'It's about the case. Pat Grady, in the coastguard office told me he received a second call that night.'

'The night of the murder?'

'The same.'

He went silent for a minute. When he spoke again, his tone had improved.

'Why didn't he tell my constable?' he said.

'I don't know. Maybe because no-one takes Pat seriously and they never give him a chance to finish what he's trying to say.'

'I have seen paint dry faster than Pat Grady finishing a sentence.'

I laughed.

'He told me the second call was made from a phone box too. Do you still have the prints?'

'Is the Pope a catholic?'

'I've got to go. Let me know if there are any developments.'

'Of course not.'

I grinned and hung up. I looked up to find Harry staring at me. A shadow passed over his face.

'Calling your boyfriend?' he said.

I'm pretty sure he didn't mean it to sound the way it did, but I felt accused. Instead of explaining about the breaks in the case, I just nodded and went back into the house. I should have been thrilled at our haul, but I couldn't relax. The atmosphere had grown toxic again somehow. I guess when two sides in a relationship feel it being threatened, no one knows how to back down. I couldn't let it stew. Our entire relationship depended on trust, both business and other, and I couldn't risk it breaking down. I forced the issue.

Harry had left two chairs on the front lawn for loading into the van, and I plonked myself down in one. The next time he came out of the house carrying a hallstand, I pointed at the other.

'We need to talk,' I said.

'Didn't we already try that?' he said.

'Bear with me. It's important.'

He sat down, his arms and legs crossed away from me. Talk about poor body language.

'Talk then.'

'I rang George because I had an important new lead in the case. I bumped into Pat Grady from the coastguard office last night, and he told me he received a second call about Ed's boat on the night of the murder.'

Harry's eyes opened wide.

'A second call? Do we know who from?'

'No, but it was someone who knew how to use an old telephone box. I should have called George first thing, but I forgot, and that's why I called him now. However, there is something I didn't tell him…'

I let my voice trail off, and watched as he unfolded his limbs and leaned forward.

'What?' he said.

'Mouse's friend Goose can get us a copy of the CCTV from the night of the murder, so we can try to eliminate Roz and Ed from the investigation.'

'But that's fantastic news. Why didn't you tell me?'

'Because I was grumpy about Emily.'

'Jealous?'

'Yes. Is that wrong? You're jealous about George.'

He shrugged.

'Come over here,' he said, patting his lap.

'Seriously? I weigh as much as a sofa.'

'A fridge. But I can take it.'

I crossed the space in a heartbeat, threw myself onto his lap and swung my legs over the arm of the chair. He grabbed his throat and pretended to be fighting for breath. I turned to look into his eyes. They twinkled at me and I felt myself leaning closer, my hair hanging down over his face. I could feel his heart thunder under my chest and his breath on my neck. He pushed the strands of my hair out of the way and took my face in his hands. I think my heart stopped for a second as we gazed into each other's eyes. Did he kiss me, or did I kiss him? All I know is his lips were soft and warm, and when I opened my eyes, his were still shut.

Chapter 25

Harry whistled as he finished loading the van, a sure sign he felt happy. I tried not to act like a soppy teenager, but I couldn't escape the feeling of that first kiss. I tried to remember if I had ever anticipated a kiss more than that one. Would there be more? Had we made a massive mistake?

'Are you going to stand there all day?' he said, grinning.

I came back down to earth and blushed.

'Sorry. Just daydreaming.'

'About me, I hope.'

'About cake.'

'Good plan. Let's raid the Vintage.'

We stopped outside the shop to unload our booty and Mouse came out to help us bring it inside. He ran his hand along the maple-topped table and sat on one of the stools.

'They look like something out of Playschool,' he said.

'Aren't they great? People will pay loads for them.'

'Like the fish?'

'Shut up and carry them inside, clever clogs.'

Harry sniggered.

'Have you sold many fish yet?' he said.

'Not one. Unless you count the fish Lexi took home. Which reminds me, she hasn't paid me for it yet.'

I went upstairs to make us all a coffee and raid the cake stand. An uncut coffee and walnut cake, which I didn't remember ordering, graced the display, begging for me to chop two big slices out of it. An exquisite card perched on top which proclaimed it had originated from Ghita's Kitchen. I wondered when Ghita had started making cakes. Her curries and Indian cooking made people feel faint with delight, but I hadn't realised she could also bake.

'Do you know anything about this cake?' I said.

'Oh, it's Ghita's new enterprise,' said Mouse. 'I told her she could try out her flavours in the café. If people like them, she will make more. Maybe we could sell whole cakes if people want them?'

'Maybe we could,' I said.

I put the slices on plates and took a nibble from one. Celestial orchestras played on my tongue. Honestly, not to exaggerate, it tasted like nectar of the Gods, nutty with latte icing. I warmed the milk for the coffee and had another nibble of the delicious cake.

Lexi and Amanda were not in the office, so I couldn't drop any hints about the payment for the taxidermy fish. They had another interview with an environmental project to do the customer research and marketing to the stakeholders. David's death had certainly generated a great deal of publicity for Lexi's consultancy. Mouse had also benefited, as Amanda couldn't cope with all the extra work generated. He got to spend more time with Amanda, so he blossomed in his new role. What if Lexi wanted to take him away? I tried not to dwell on this unpleasant thought.

Harry took the van to the car park and came back with a smirk on his face. My heart started racing again as I caught his eye. I deliberately sat on the other side of Mouse to Harry so I wouldn't have to control my surging feelings. If Mouse thought we had finally got together, he would be over the top happy, and I couldn't be sure what would come next. I still had to tell George to back off, and I didn't see that as an easy option. Luckily, Ghita's cake distracted Harry, sending him into paroxysms of ecstasy. He licked his fingers one by one. I tried not to watch. Mouse cleared his throat.

'I made some progress too while you were away,' he said, opening his laptop. 'You'll never guess who did an environmental degree course at Hull fifteen years ago?'

He spun the laptop around so we could see the screen.

'Blimey,' said Harry. 'That's a turn up for the books.'

'His surname wasn't de Frontenac at all,' I said.

'Nope. May I present the undergrad student, David Foster, of Kingston upon Hull? His father is a painter and his mother a school dinner lady. No aristocratic roots. No public-school education. Frank Burgess got one thing right anyway. David de Frontenac didn't exist. He was a fraud.'

Mouse showed us a page of student photographs. David's shone out, clear as day, fifteen years younger, but the same handsome, arrogant face sneering into the camera. I looked through the other photographs and one girl caught my eye. She stared out from the page. Her blue eyes were expressionless. I felt like I had seen her somewhere before, but I couldn't put my finger on it. Perhaps I had met her with Lexi somewhere? And then I saw another face I recognised. Well, not recognised exactly, but I knew who it was.

'Look at her,' I said to Harry. 'Does her face ring a bell?'

'Oh my days. Freya Burgess? She looks just like him. She must be Frank's daughter, poor thing.'

'No wonder he didn't trust David. I bet she had a grandstand view of his behaviour. I think we need to talk to Burgess again.'

'What will I do with this page?' said Mouse.

'Can you send the link to George?' I said.

'No,' said Mouse. 'He'll arrest me for hacking.'

'Naughty, naughty,' said Harry.

'Can you print out a copy of the photos for me? I think Lexi knows more than she's letting on too. It will be hard for her to deny if she sees his mugshot. When she went to see George on the first day after David's death, she claimed to have known him all his life. Unless that's also a lie. Or maybe she knows about the name change, but she doesn't want to say so. I'll corner her when she gets back from the interview.'

'Sure, I'll do that now. I wanted to get a sandwich anyway. Shall I get something for you?'

'No thanks. I'm happy with cake,' said Harry, and he winked at me.

Mouse caught my expression, and he raised his eyebrows in inquiry. I pretended not to see him.

'Are you two hiding something?' he said.

'What makes you say that?' I said.

He shrugged.

'I'll get the photos printed out,' he said.

When Mouse had left, Harry moved to sit right beside me, our thighs touching.

'Are we hiding something?' he said.

'Mouse knows how I feel about you.'

'And do you?'

A clang rang out as Lexi and Amanda came in. Never was saved by the bell so appropriate. I didn't know why I couldn't decide. I had taken a trip to outer space when Harry kissed me. He was everything George wasn't, but still I doubted myself. I now knew why people stayed in marriages that had been over for years. Change is terrifying and depression makes you doubt yourself.

'Can we take a rain check please? I'd like to do this conversation when we've got some time and privacy,' I said.

'Fair enough. You should talk to Lexi as soon as possible. And I'll tell Emily we need to speak to Frank again about his daughter. Romance will have to wait.'

He pecked me on the forehead and left, waving hello and goodbye to Lexi and Amanda as he passed by them. I waited for them at the door of the office.

'How was the interview?' I said. 'Did you get the contract?'

'We'll know next week. I expect we'll be finished here soon as well. We need to talk about Mouse. He shouldn't be stuck here in this backwater all his life,' said Lexi.

She lowered her voice for the last part about Mouse. I nodded as if in agreement, but I had no intention of letting my stepson leave without a fight.

'I think you need to speak to me about David first,' I said.

She faked a yawn.

'Honestly, can't we let sleeping dogs lie, or even die?'

'I'm afraid not. You've been lying to the police about David and where he comes from.'

Amanda let out a gasp, but she turned it into a cough when I glanced at her. What did she know about this? We had been barking up the wrong tree completely here. George and his team were preparing a case against Roz and Ed, but they only had half the story. We needed to find out how Frank Burgess knew about David. And if they had a past that should be investigated. And what were Lexi and Amanda hiding?

'You mean his name? Okay, I admit it. I didn't want to betray his confidence if I didn't have to,' said Lexi.

'But what about his actual family? Someone should tell them about his death.'

Lexi sighed.

'You don't understand. His family thinks he's dead. It will be quite a shock for them to realise he's been alive all this time. Do you really think we need to tell the police?'

'Somebody shot him dead, and my friends are being held for the murder. Of course, the police need to know. This could change the direction of the inquiry.'

'If you ask me, it's pretty obvious they're the ones who murdered David, but I'll go to the station and talk to George.'

'I don't understand how David got accepted by high society after doing his degree. I presume that's when he changed his name?'

'I helped him choose it.'

'Why?'

'He had charisma and animal magnetism, and I fancied him like mad. He was my project.'

'But didn't he stick out in the beginning? Surely people could tell he wasn't one of them.'

'Are you saying he was infra dig? No, darling. People in our circle accepted him because of his glamour and intelligence. He slotted into our lives as if he'd always been there. He made the occasional mistake in the beginning, but he took private elocution lessons throughout university.'

'Did you know about this?' I asked Amanda, whose mouth had opened in shock and was still not closed.

'The bastard,' she said. 'I knew there was something funny about him, but I couldn't put my finger on it. I guess his charm blinded me. To think I let him…'

She shivered theatrically.

'Do you want me to go with you to see George?' I said to Lexi.

'No. Don't bother. I know the way.'

Chapter 26

To my surprise, Frank Burgess agreed to meet us the next afternoon at the end of the pier in the Ocean Café. On condition we stumped up for a cream tea. It seemed like a small price to pay to find out if David's past had caused his murder after George rebuffed Lexi's revelation with a demand for evidence. This was his usual mantra, and one I recognised. I had to admit we had zero evidence that David's change of name had anything to do with his murder, but I had a strong gut feeling about it. George told Lexi he had bullets and a gun at the forensics lab, and they trumped any feelings about the case, gut or otherwise.

Both Roz and Ed were being held on remand, having been charged with murder. Since they both claimed to be guilty, the police had every right to hold them. Roz had refused to see me again, and Ed would see no one, so we were at a stalemate. I sent Roz comfort parcels and cheery notes, but I didn't receive any acknowledgement. We had reached a stalemate as far as they were concerned. Their determination to take the blame for each other made it impossible to help them.

The one good thing about our discovery of the truth about David de Frontenac, or at least the beginnings of it, was the effect it had on Ghita. She swapped sides immediately and delivered a stream of delicious cakes to the Vintage to keep our spirits up. I much preferred to buy them from her than from the franchise bakery, so we were both happy. We decided we would nominate a cake of the month for the café and ask people to vote for their favourites to feature in the coming month. Since she had started with a coffee and walnut cake, we installed that as the first choice. Our regular customers loved Ghita's baking, and soon the café buzzed with them and their friends.

Since Harry needed to deliver the excess stock from the Swedish house to the London warehouse he worked with, I asked Mouse to come to the Ocean café to meet Frank Burgess. We walked out to sea along the boards of the pier at high tide. I always enjoyed the feeling of walking out over the water and into the breakers crashing against the legs of the pier. The ozone made my appetite keener and I could fit more air in my lungs, or so it seemed to me. Mouse loved to look over the side and try to spot the quicksilver flashes of shoals of ravenous fish who came inshore to eat everything they could find.

We entered through the double doors of the art deco entrance hall and then pushed the second set to enter the inner sanctum, a large tall room shaped like the prow of an ocean liner. The waitress found us a table to one side of the room where we could watch the diners, as they ate and talked and scraped their cutlery against their plates. Frank Burgess turned up fifteen minutes late with a younger woman I recognised from her photo, Freya Burgess. I had to hand it to him. He didn't do things by half. I noticed he had squeezed himself back into his shiny suit and even combed what remained of his hair. His daughter wore a dress suggestive of Laura Ashley circa 1990. He had produced a female clone, in both body shape and facial structure, but the smile on her face when she saw Mouse immediately endeared her to me. He had that effect on women.

'Hello,' I said. 'You must be Freya.'

She looked surprised.

'Did Dad tell you that? He never mentions me to anyone.'

Mouse kicked me under the table and rolled his eyes. What an idiot. I nearly gave the game away in one.

'I think I saw a picture of you in his office,' I said.

Frank nodded, although I could see that my knowledge had mystified him too.

'Shall I order us some cream teas?' I said.

'With all the trimmings,' said Frank.

'Absolutely.'

The table soon heaved with finger sandwiches, scones and clotted cream, petit fours, macaroons and many sweet delicacies. I'm not sure there is anything quite like an English afternoon tea for the pleasurable sugar rush it gives you. Frank Burgess ate his way through a positive mountain of goodies before sitting back and patting his plump tummy.

'Emily told me you want to know more about David de Frontenac. She said you had discovered his real name?' he said.

'David Foster? Yes, and I believe you knew it too.'

'Not me. My daughter. She went to university with that scoundrel, didn't you Freya?'

'Unfortunately, we did the same degree, environmental sciences at Hull.'

'What was he like?' I asked.

'He started out like all of us. A normal student doing a degree. Studying and partying with us. Then he hooked up with Hazel.'

'Hazel who?' said Mouse, and I knew he meant to look her up as soon as we got back to the office.

'Hazel Smith. She came from an aristocratic family, or at least she had an upper-class accent and attitude. I don't know if it was real or not. Anyway, David copied her. He took elocution lessons and hung around on the fringes of their groups, copying mannerisms and learning about the season and so on.'

'What happened?' I said.

'By the time we graduated, he had transformed himself into a posh bloke. He had been accepted into upper-class circles and he disappeared off the radar.'

'What happened to Hazel?' said Mouse.

'He dumped her. I guess she had served her purpose by opening a crack in the door. She came from an old aristocratic family herself, but he didn't need her anymore.'

'She must have been devastated,' I said.

'All I know is that she never turned up to the final exams.'

'She didn't get her degree?' said Mouse.

'No, she just disappeared.'

'What a bastard. He didn't change much. How did you know he had come down here?' I said.

'I saw his photograph in the local paper and told Dad. He thought we could persuade him to give up his fight for the kelp forest if he was threatened with exposure.'

Frank nodded in approval.

'Blackmail?' said Mouse.

'Sort of. But he deserved it,' said Frank. 'I told him to drop the application for the MPA or I would expose him as a fraud.'

'So, you didn't kill him then?' I said.

'Don't be ridiculous. How would that prevent the council from granting the MPA? I thought the combination of David's past, and my sister on the council could save me from going under.'

'What will you do now?' said Mouse.

'A mate of mine has hired my dredgers for a contract, so I'll be all right for the time being. I'll get by. I always have.'

Freya patted his hand and squeezed it.

'Will you let me know if you find Hazel?' she said. 'I'd love to get in contact with her again. She wasn't like him.'

'I don't like to speak ill of the dead, but he had it coming,' said Frank. 'And if that couple, the Murrays, killed him, they had their reasons.'

Chapter 27

The revelations about David Foster did not provide me with any ammunition in the fight to free Roz and Ed. If anything, it made me understand just how ruthless David had been, and believe Roz's story of the assault all the more. David didn't care who he hurt, or how much. This was driven home by his heartless treatment of Hazel. Mouse had tried to trace her, but she too had vanished from the surface of the planet as if she never existed. I couldn't believe how easy it was to reinvent yourself or disappear completely before the days of the internet. Now, as far as I could see, everything you ever did would be recorded for thousands of years, including, in some cases, what you ate for breakfast. I still liked to look through the photograph albums of my childhood schooldays and holidays when I felt nostalgic. Would future generations scroll through people's breakfasts and selfies? How incredibly depressing.

Car boot sale season had reached full swing, and I tried to go to the Shoreham Flyover version every Sunday. The ground conditions could be a little treacherous, but most people didn't have any concept of the value of the goods they were flogging, which made the sale a great place to find bargains for the shop. I took Mouse with me a few times, when I could persuade him out of bed at seven thirty to make the quick trip along the coast to the field. Unlike Harry, Mouse liked to learn the value of things and followed me around, assiduously picking up nuggets of information about 1960s and 70s glassware and kitchenalia. Soon he felt confident enough to accept a handful of notes and set out by himself down one row of tables while I scouted the other. Since most things were in the one-to-five-pound range, he could do limited damage to my finances if he made a mistake, and he quickly became more than competent.

When we got back to the shop with our hauls, it gave him another reason to spend hours trawling the internet. He priced every article he could find on the net, and learned more as he searched. I praised and encouraged him as much as I could. His enthusiasm infected me and we became quite a team. I no longer worried about letting him off the leash at fairs and felt excited at the prospect of seeing what he turned up. It's a pity George couldn't see Mouse like this, his eyes bright with excitement as he brought me Bakelite treasures purchased for a song. George still thought his son was a layabout and a waste of space. I think the shame of having to bail Mouse out of prison for carjacking had not yet dissipated. Knowing George, he would never let Mouse forget it. I felt a lot less charitable about George when I considered his treatment of his son.

The stock we rescued from the car boot sales gave the shop a new lease of life as customers poured in to purchase our finds. Mouse had not had time to pursue his search for Hazel Smith, as he worked full time in the

Vintage and pricing our new stock. I waited for Flo to let me know the results of the forensics on the bullets and the Murrays' Enfield revolver, but, as usual, the lab in Wantage had a waiting time of one month. I mourned for Roz, stuck in the women's prison, determined not to implicate her husband for a murder neither of them had committed. But who had? I didn't feel any closer to the truth. Hazel Smith might hold the key to unlocking the case, but we also needed the CCTV feed to establish the identity of the person who visited the harbour on the night of the murder. I wanted to find out why the police were so sure it was Roz.

Goose kept putting Mouse off when he asked about progress in obtaining the digital copy for that night. He prevaricated and didn't answer his phone, giving the impression of taking his time. I wondered if he really had the right contacts in the tightknit sector to extract it from the owner. I tried to distract myself by scrubbing forty-year-old fly excrement off glassware and tea sets, but even with the best will in the world, it's not exactly a riveting occupation. Just when I had accepted defeat an email from Goose pinged in Mouse's inbox with a link to a file on Dropbox. Mouse transferred the file to my account before telling me it had arrived. He came downstairs to tell me about it. He put his finger to his lips before whispering in my ear.

'It's here? Why didn't you tell me?' I hissed at him.

'Because I think we should watch it at home first, and maybe get Harry and Ghita over to see it with us. We are the only people who think Roz is innocent. I don't want people gloating over the video.'

By people, he meant Lexi. She had always been sure of Roz and Ed's guilt, and to be fair to her, so had the police. I wondered if her background made her more likely to trust authority so implicitly. I sympathised with Mouse. He had always got on well with Roz. I hadn't told him about the assault because I didn't want to upset him even more. Actually, I hadn't told anyone. Roz had asked me not to, and I would respect her wishes unless it became vital to tell the truth.

So that evening we downloaded the video onto my laptop at home and watched it with Harry. The video ran for only about twenty seconds and I held my breath. The feed was black and white and somewhat pixelated because of the darkness of the night, and we watched in complete silence as someone came into view and passed under a streetlamp and walked away. I couldn't see the person's face, but they had a mop of light-coloured curls and were wearing a diaphanous dress which wafted as they walked. Was it Roz? The visual signals told me so, but I doubted my eyes. Something didn't add up, but I couldn't figure out what.

'What do you think?' I said.

'It looks like Roz,' said Harry. 'Look at the hair.'

Mouse played and replayed the video. A feeling of dread replaced my doubt. Then the doorbell rang. I went to answer it and Ghita stood outside.

'Can I see it?' she said.

'You may, but it's not good news,' I said. 'Do you want a glass of wine?'

'I'd rather see the video first.'

I sat on the sofa and sipped my drink, while Mouse and Harry keyed up the video for Ghita to watch. She gazed at the screen and made them replay a few times as the figure walked past the lamppost. She shook her head. I waited with bated breath for her verdict. To my surprise, she turned to us with a massive smile.

'That's not Roz,' she said.

'But the hair and the dress?' I said.

'It's someone pretending to be Roz,' said Ghita, curling her lip just a little.

'But how do you know?' said Mouse.

'That person is way shorter than Roz. When I walk down that street with her, she always makes me walk beside the lamppost because of the hanging basket. I'm small enough to walk underneath it, but she has to duck. The person in the video is my height. I don't care how dark it is. That's not Roz. Someone is trying to frame her.'

I squeaked with excitement and pulled Ghita in for a group hug.

'You wonderful woman,' I said. 'You may have just got Roz out of jail. Do you want to tell George about the height thing?'

'It would be my great pleasure. I'm sure they'll send guys with measuring tapes down there, but they'll just find out I'm right.'

'What have we got so far?' I said.

'David de Frontenac was a fraud who dumped his long-term girlfriend when he adopted his persona,' said Mouse. 'We have to find her. She could easily have framed Roz.'

'But what motive would she have? If she wanted to kill David, she could have done it without framing anyone. She has been AWOL for years. Why bother?' said Harry.

'We need to find her, regardless,' I said. 'Mouse, you've got the skills.'

'Okay, I'll try again. There's bound to be a file on her somewhere. I can get her name and address.'

'Good plan. If you can find a phone number for her or her parents, that would be wonderful,' I said.

'She'd be the right age for the murderer,' said Harry. 'Remember, the person who did this called in from a phone box. I don't know anyone below the age of thirty who knows how to use a dial-up phone, especially one you put coins in.'

'What about the gun? And the wig and dress? They could be anywhere,' said Ghita.

I sighed.

'I don't know, but let's see if we can find out about Hazel Smith first. She might be the key person in this mystery.'

When Ghita and Harry had left, I called George, but he didn't answer. I guessed Sharon had come home from her sister's house and she didn't like him talking to me. I sent him a text telling him I had important information for him concerning the case. Then I turned off my phone and went to bed.

Chapter 28

George rang the doorbell first thing in the morning and I rewarded him by appearing at my front door in my ratty old dressing gown with bed-hair and bad breath. He raised an eyebrow at my dishevelled appearance, but swallowed whatever comment had occurred to him.

'You've made a break in the case?' he said. 'Out with it. I'm in a hurry.'

'Actually, I may have broken your case,' I said, smirking. 'I watched a copy of the CCTV footage of the woman on her way to the boat on the night of the murder.'

'I won't ask you where you got hold of that, but it's not illegal. Did you see something we missed?'

'The woman in the footage is not Roz Murray. From her height, I'm still assuming it's a woman, but anyway it's not Roz.'

'Another gut feeling? Seriously, you called me over for this nugget?'

'Bear with me. Roz is nearly five feet ten inches. The woman in your footage is about five foot two.'

'And how do you know that?'

'Because she doesn't have to duck under the hanging basket on the lamppost. Send your technicians over to measure it. Or try walking Roz underneath it. You'll see.'

'So, we're back to square one?'

'I think so. Ed is only claiming to be the murderer to take the heat off Roz. To tell the truth, it's pretty obvious someone is trying to frame one or both of them. Someone who knows how they feel about each other and is trying to take advantage of it.'

George rolled his eyes.

'We should get the forensics on the gun back today. I've a feeling that gun hasn't been fired since V.E. day.'

'We're looking into something else. I don't know if it's anything yet, but I promise to tell you if we find out anything important. As you would say, there is absolutely no evidence, only hunches right now.'

'That's more than I've got. Let me know if it's something we should look into. Have a nice day, and thanks.'

'You can stay for breakfast.'

'I'll get a bacon butty in the canteen.'

And he left me standing in the street looking like death warmed up. I backed into the house and shut the door. Behind me, Hades yowled about his hunger and my neglect. I sighed and made for the kitchen where I took out one of his expensive pouches of gourmet cat food. He had lately decided only the best would do and turned his nose up at everything else. I swear he did it on purpose.

I looked at my watch and found it wasn't even eight o'clock yet. On a whim, I decided I would go up to Hull and do some digging. I shook Mouse awake to ask him to mind the shop.

'You don't have to go to Hull,' he said. 'I found the address of Hazel Smith's parents. Their house is just outside King's Colne, a small village in Essex. I'll text you it to you and you can put the post code into your GPS.'

'King's Colne?' I couldn't think why I had heard of it before, but an old memory lurked somewhere in the recesses of my brain. 'That's a lot closer. I could be there in time for lunch. I'll get dressed and shoot off straight away. Ring me if you find out anything else.'

'I'm going back to bed.'

I got ready and gulped down a cup of tea, my excitement rising. I hadn't done anything like this since my days as an investigative journalist. Would my Spidey skills still work? I had become more confident since my divorce from George, but the doubts still lingered. However, this was no time to be wimping out. I grabbed a banana and the car keys, and headed out to the Mini. I had been so excited by the prospect of a field trip I forgot to take the rush hour into account, and I soon found myself snarled up in slow traffic. The calories from the banana soon dissipated and my stomach let me know it disapproved of my impromptu diet.

When I got to King's Colne, I headed for the nearest pub in the hope of a ploughman's or some chicken and chips. The King's Head sat on a side road off the high street. It had a shambolic air as the foundations on one side had sunk, making the walls lurch slightly. The sign swung in the wind, creaking like the rigging on a schooner. I entered a warm, muggy lounge bar with cheap furniture and sticky tables. I almost left again, but the smell of food lured me to the bar where I ordered goujons of chicken with chips in a basket. The landlady nodded in approval and pulled me half a pint of cider. The other clients were seated at the window tables and I felt obliged to engage in some polite chit-chat while I waited for my food.

'How old is this pub?' I said, looking around at the mildew on the ceiling and the threadbare carpets.

'Even older than me, ducks,' said the landlady, laughing. 'I've worked here for thirty years.'

'I don't believe it. You've hardly got a wrinkle.'

'Pickled, dearie. Much better than Botox.'

'Do you know the Smith family?'

'I don't think so. Do you have their first names? Or their ages?'

'I think their daughter Hazel would be about 35 or 40 now.'

She went rigid at the mention of Hazel's name and she shut her eyes.

'Hazel?' she said.

'I have a photograph if that helps,' I said, rummaging through my handbag.

She put a hand on my arm and shook her head at me.

'I don't need a photo to remember Hazel. She started coming in here when she was about fifteen. I wouldn't serve her, though. I knew how old she was.'

'And do you know where she is now?'

She tilted her head on one side.

'You don't know?'

'I'm sorry. That's why I came. I'm trying to find out what happened to her after University.'

'He murdered her, he did.'

'Who?'

'That David Foster.'

'She was murdered?'

'He didn't stab her, but he killed her as sure as sticking a knife in her heart. She committed suicide when he dumped her before the Leavers' Ball at Hull.'

'Oh, my goodness, I'm so sorry. I didn't know.'

She wiped her eyes with a bar towel.

'Fifteen years have passed, but I still expect her to pop in and have a vodka and tonic, even now.'

'Do her parents still live in the village?'

'Her father does, but her mother died of a broken heart. He remarried. She's all right. Brassy, but loads of money.'

I felt the hairs on my arms stand up. King's Colne. Of course. The village Lexi's father lived in.

'She called herself Hazel Smith at University,' I said. 'Was that her real surname?'

'Hazel didn't want anyone to know she came from a posh family. They were down on their luck, so she dropped the double-barrelled surname.'

'Burlington-Smythe?'

'That's right. How did you know if—'

'It's a long story. I came to ask her about David, but I guess it's a wasted journey.'

'Why did you want to know?'

'Someone murdered him a few weeks ago. The police can't find a motive.'

196

'I'd have killed him myself if he showed up here. That man had no heart.'

'Did you ever meet him?'

'No, he never showed his face around here. But I think her sister met him once.'

'Her sister?'

'Alexandra.'

A grubby teenager emerged from the kitchen and shoved a basket of chicken goujons and chips at me. The landlady smiled.

'Here's your food. Ketchup? Mayonnaise?' she said, back to business as usual, as if we had never spoken about the past.

'Both please.'

I took my basket with sachets of sauces balanced on top and a fork clutched in my hand, and I headed for the nearest table. I couldn't believe what I had found out. No wonder Lexi had an ambiguous attitude towards David. But what the hell was she doing working with him? Had he realised who she was? It made little sense. I pulled a sachet open and squirted ketchup all over the table. Now I knew why they were all sticky. I tried to eat my lunch, but I found it hard to swallow. I asked the landlady if she would make me a pot of tea because I couldn't face a sweet cider.

I pushed the basket to one side and took out my phone. I noticed three missed calls from Mouse. Why hadn't I heard the ring tone? I dialled his number, and he picked up almost immediately.

'You've got to come home,' he said. 'It's Amanda.'

'What happened?'

'The police arrested her. They found the wig and the dress in her desk drawer. I, I, I…'

'It's okay. I'm finished here. I'll be home as soon as I can.'

'What did you find out?'

'You won't believe it. I'll tell you when I get back.'

Chapter 29

I tried not to break the speed limit on my way home, and luckily my Mini had got to the stage where driving fast meant over forty miles an hour. How had the police known about the wig and the dress in Amanda's desk drawer? And why would she be keeping it there? Amanda struck me as being more intelligent than most. I couldn't imagine she would have committed a murder and then hidden the evidence in the desk she used for work. A little voice in my head told me who might have done this and I couldn't shut it out. Lexi had just as much motive and opportunity, and she could have framed Ed and Roz. But how on earth did she lift David into the bulkhead storage space? Did she have help?

Mouse waited for me in the Vintage. I hardly recognised my shop. I'd never seen the place so clean. Stress had brought out his need for control over his environment, probably a deep-seated reaction to losing his mother so young. The coffee machine gleamed and all the table tops had fresh wax. Then I noticed the police tape still hanging from the office door making me feel as if I was having some sort of out-of-body experience. I blinked twice, but it stayed there. Mouse came down the stairs two at a time and stood speechless at the bottom, shaking with emotion. I opened my arms, and he fell into them, burying his face in my shoulder. He emitted some guttural sobs before he sniffed and pulled away.

'They took her to the station,' he said, wiping tears from his cheeks. 'I can't believe it.'

'Don't worry. After my visit to King's Colne today, I'm sure she didn't do this. What did the police say?'

'They received a tip off from a member of the public.'

'Again? I have a feeling I know who made that call. She's been right in front of us all the time. Where's Lexi?'

'She showed the police some correspondence she'd had with David about Amanda, and they asked her to come to the station with them.'

'Did you see what the emails contained?'

'No, but I heard them saying something about blackmail.'

'Blackmail? Who blackmailed who?'

'I don't know. We have to help her. She's my…'

'I know, sweetheart. I like her too. We need to stay calm and review the evidence.'

'But they took away her computer, and Lexi's,' said Mouse.

'It's not the end of the world. Lexi printed out most of the project documents and emails. We'll have to go back to the nineties and read pieces of paper instead of a screen. Why don't you gather everything together in a box and we'll take them home? I'll get Harry and Ghita over. We'll review everything from the beginning and see if we can find any clues.'

But Harry had gone to see an old aunt of his in the East End, and Ghita had a mysterious appointment which she couldn't or wouldn't change, so Mouse and I found ourselves on our own. I reheated some lasagne in the oven and we crisped up a frozen garlic bread to eat. Why is reheated food so delicious? We devoured everything, and it didn't take long before we were running the bread across our plates to wipe up the last of the sauce. Then I poured myself a glass of red wine and we sat on the sofa with the box between our feet. Hades approached the box and got in. He had a smug look on his face as I reached in and tried to extract a document. Then he scratched me. I yelped and tipped him out, but he tried to get in again.

'Honestly,' I said, sucking my finger. 'Sometimes I don't know why I bother.'

I fetched a pouch of his favourite food and emptied it into his bowl on the floor beside the box.

'I already fed him,' said Mouse.

'I need to keep my fingers,' I said. 'I don't have time for this.'

We took a document each and began to read. Mouse made a song and dance about having to read on paper instead of a screen, but soon he was absorbed in reading an article about saving the oceans. It featured a flattering photograph of David, but when had he ever looked less than perfect? I guess the night Roz knocked him flying, he must have been mussed up a little. Would the police release her and Ed now that they had Amanda in custody? I tried to remember normal procedure, but this case had been anything but normal. I could picture George getting exasperated as his careful logging of the evidence against Roz and Ed got scrubbed out with one tip to the hotline. Sharon would have to produce something more soothing than reheated lasagne to calm him down this evening.

I picked up a statement of accounts done by Amanda and tried to spot any suspicious entries. I had a pet hate for accounts, even though I'm generally good at numbers, but I could spot an irregularity at ten paces. People murdered other people for two main reasons: love and money. An environmental charity had many donations coming in. Had some of them gone astray? I hoped Amanda didn't turn out to have a fatal flaw. Mouse did not give his heart away easily. I couldn't imagine his reaction if Amanda had been stealing. But what if David took advantage of his position to pocket funds? I considered that much more likely. Had Amanda found out? And blackmailed him. Or had she discovered his real name? David seemed to me to be a prime candidate for blackmail.

My rapid perusal of the accounts didn't flag up any major financial irregularities. The accounts did not balance, but I couldn't put my hand on the Bible and swear that Second Home's accounts had no mistakes in them. I got the feeling that either someone had forgotten to add in all the expenses, or small amounts had been syphoned off from time to time. It hardly seemed like enough to kill for. Maybe enough to fire someone for though. I put the file to one side and selected some handwritten notes from a stakeholders' meeting. I recognised Lexi's scrawl down the margins, mostly insults about stakeholders and their dress sense. Nothing important. Time ticked by without either of us having a

Eureka moment. Mouse got up to play with Hades for a while before sitting back down. His deep sighs told me we were reaching the bottom of the box with no major revelations. I really wanted to exonerate Amanda, but I could find nothing nefarious to show Lexi had a plan to murder David, either.

I picked up a copy of the final presentation Lexi used to convince stakeholders about the sense of regrowing the kelp forest offshore at Seacastle. I meant to chuck it on the already read pile, but I couldn't resist flicking through to see the great photographs of the fish one more time. That morning on the dive had been magical. I could still picture Harry's tattoo. I wished I could be brave enough to finish what we started. The feeling of his lips on mine still haunted my thoughts.

'Ahem. You're daydreaming,' said Mouse. 'Either that, or you have a thing about bream hatchlings. Mind you, that photograph is fantastic. Who took it?'

I looked at the photo again. It resembled a real-life version of *Finding Nemo* with the little fish hiding among the thick fronds of kelp. I wondered what on earth they made of these weird humans swimming among them? They probably thought we were plump seals. The photographer had captured the moment perfectly. And then the penny dropped.

'David did,' I said. 'I remember him showing it to me on board Ed's boat the day of the dive.'

'But I thought David used his phone to take photographs that day. I stuck that photograph into the presentation myself, from the kelp project's cloud storage. But I had no idea it was one of David's,' said Mouse.

'But the police haven't found David's mobile yet, so how did the photos get into the cloud storage of the kelp project? Who uploaded them from David's phone between the dive and his murder? It may have been David, but if he didn't do it, who did? When you combine that mystery with what I learned today, I expect Lexi will move to the top of the suspect list.'

'Whoa! You haven't told me about your trip yet. Obviously, it wasn't a waste of time.'

I slapped my forehead.

'The opposite. I can't believe I haven't told you.'

'We've been quite preoccupied. What did you find out?'

'Well, for a start, David wasn't the only one using a false name.'

'Are you serious?'

'It's hardly credible, is it? Nobody is who they claimed to be. Take a guess at Hazel Smith's real surname. It rhymes with hive.'

'You're not serious. She's related to Lexi?'

'She was her sister. And, I'm sorry to relate, she killed herself after David dumped her before the Leavers' Ball at Hull University.'

'Poor girl. That's awful. But it's a hell of a motive for Lexi. How could she bear to be near David after that?'

'Perhaps she planned this all along, and just waited for the perfect opportunity.'

'But why did he work with her at all if she was Hazel's sister?'

'My guess is he didn't know that. He had no reason for suspecting Hazel of using a false name, because he used one for the opposite reason that she did.'

'He used de Frontenac to pretend to be posh, and she used Smith to pretend not to be. That's so weird.'

'I think we can safely say we have circumstantial evidence to give George now, which points at Lexi, not at Amanda. But how will we persuade him to get his techies to gain access to the project's cloud storage?'

'I'll have a word with him. He still listens to me,' I said.

'He's not much of a detective without you, is he?'

I smiled.

'That's a little unfair. We worked together on cases for ten years. It takes a while to break those ties. He relied on me as a sounding board and now he's stranded between the two of us. I don't know if Sharon has much interest in helping him with policing.'

'I don't know if he'll ever stop needing you.'

'That's his problem.'

Chapter 30

The next morning, I texted George with the offer of breakfast and updates on the case. My telephone pinged almost immediately, making me grin. It seemed the poor man was still on a diet. To my surprise, Mouse dragged himself out of bed and took a shower. He even put on one of his favourite t-shirts. We laid the table in the kitchen and shooed Hades out into the garden. He hissed and spat at me, but Mouse just picked him up by the scruff of the neck and carried him into the bramble patch.

'It's for your own good,' he said.

We locked the cat flap so he couldn't force his way back in. George hated cats and there was no point in antagonising him. The doorbell rang and Mouse went to answer it while I went back into the kitchen and put the eggs in to boil. I heard Mouse welcoming George, followed by a grunt I recognised. I rolled my eyes. George never made the slightest attempt to reconcile with his son, despite Mouse turning over a new leaf, after his rocky start. He constantly found reasons to disparage him in front of other people, a habit I tried to break by disagreeing every time. George came into the kitchen, his brow furrowed, and gave me a peck on the cheek. I ignored his sulk and put the bread into the toaster.

'This case has more red herrings than the fish market,' said George. 'We've got a woman called Amanda Grant under arrest at the station. I'm led to understand she's Alexandra Burlington-Smythe's secretary?'

'I think you'll find she's the P.A. and bookkeeper,' I said. 'Have you released Roz and Ed yet?'

'They'll both be let out today. I have no choice. There's not enough room at the station and the prison won't hold anyone who hasn't been charged.'

'That's great news. And I can help you with the overcrowding issue in the station, because Amanda Grant is also innocent.'

George rolled his eyes.

'And how do you know that?' he said. 'My team found the wig and dress in her desk drawer. Talk about being caught red-handed.'

Mouse's jaw tightened, and I shook my head at him.

'Have you found a motive yet?' I said.

He rubbed his face with his hand.

'No, but that doesn't mean she's innocent. We're searching her room for the gun today.'

'I'd check the inside of the wig cap for hairs,' I said. 'I expect they'll be blonde rather than black.'

'Why do you say that?' said George.

'Amanda is too tall to be the murderer. She is almost the same height as Roz. You're on the wrong track. It's much more likely to be Lexi who murdered David.'

'Lexi? What evidence do you have of that?'

'You told us that there was no trace of David before he set up the consultancy. Did you know David de Frontenac was a pseudonym?' said Mouse. 'Or that he used to go out with Lexi's sister, Hazel, at Hull University?'

The toast popped up in the silence that followed as the muscles in George's face danced independently of each other. I bit my lip to prevent a snort of laughter from escaping and removed the eggs from the water. I put them on the table and watched as George and Mouse opened them in an identical manner, slicing the top off with one chop of their spoons, while I buttered the toast and cut it into fingers. I was dying to point it out to them, but the tight jawlines told me to hold fire.

'Is that true?' said George.

'She killed herself after David dumped her,' I said. 'She called herself Hazel Smith, so David didn't know Lexi was her sister.'

George helped himself to a few spoons of egg and munched his way through his toast fingers.

'Lexi is a prime suspect then.'

'Their father served in the army. He could have got his hands on an army issue Enfield revolver if he wanted, and Lexi could have used it to murder David,' I said.

'I suppose you have evidence which connects her to the murder?'

'I'm pretty sure she uploaded photographs from David's phone to the project server,' said Mouse.

George sighed.

'Hacking is illegal, and the evidence is non-admissible in court. Trust you to screw up the case. Can't you do anything right?'

Mouse stood up and marched out to the sitting room where he grabbed the print-out of the presentation from the pile. He flipped through the pages and folded it open, dropping it on George's plate where is stuck on a piece of toast slathered with marmalade.

'I'm a policeman's son, not an idiot,' he said, jabbing his finger at the document. 'Tanya recognised this photograph as one David showed her on the diving trip. It was taken on David's mobile phone. The phone that is missing.'

George peeled the presentation off his toast and examined the photograph.

'How does that help me?' he said.

'If you ask Amanda for the password to their server, the techies will confirm who uploaded the photograph to the server and when. Whoever did it must have David's phone. Is that good enough evidence for you?' said Mouse.

He stomped out of the room and out into the garden. I guessed he wanted to cuddle Hades, his comfort blanket. I hoped Hades wouldn't rush back in, looking for breakfast. I tutted and refilled George's mug with tea.

'Honestly. Can't you cut the boy some slack? He's made huge strides in the last couple of years. He didn't steal a car to shame you. Teenage boys are silly, and their pre-frontal cortexes are undeveloped.'

'How come I didn't steal any cars then?'

I shrugged.

'He's your only son. The least you could do is make an attempt to get to know him again. He's desperate for your attention, you know.'

'How come you're such an expert? You never showed him any attention before we got divorced.'

His comment struck home. I swallowed an insult which sat on the tip of my tongue.

'You're right. I'm as culpable as you are, but I've changed my mind. Why can't you?'

He stood up and looked into my eyes.

'You haven't changed a bit. Since I left, you've reverted to the girl I first met. I thought Sharon offered me a new future, but now I'm missing you all the time. Mouse sees you more than I do.'

My eyes opened wide.

'Oh, my goodness. You're jealous of Mouse. I can't believe it.'

He moistened his lips.

'What if I am? Can't a man fancy his own wife?'

I took a deep breath.

'It's too late. You discarded me for a new model. I'm not your wife any more.'

'You don't believe that.'

'I do. Go to work. You need to get your techies to search for that photo on the project server. When they find it, you'll know who uploaded it and what time they did that. You'll know who has David's phone, and perhaps who is the murderer of David Foster.'

He stood up and headed towards the front door.

'Thanks for breakfast,' he said, hovering. 'Would you take me back if I made up with Mouse?'

'Absolutely not.'

Chapter 31

I didn't tell Mouse about George's proposition. Instead, I lied and told him his father had apologised. George's words had discombobulated me. Should I take him back? Did I even want him anymore? What about Harry?

'Honestly, I wasn't born yesterday,' said Mouse. 'When did my father ever apologise for anything?'

'We should get to the shop,' I said, ignoring him. 'I want to speak to Lexi before the police do.'

'Won't Dad be cross with you?'

'He's always annoyed with me. That's why we're divorced.'

We left the Mini at home and strode along the promenade. The sea was ditch green near shore, graduating to deep blue in the depths. The stems of the wind farm turbines gleamed white against the horizon. Small white-topped waves blew in sideways against the pebble banks and the palm trees leant over in the breeze. I launched the remaining crusts from the breakfast toast up into the air where the swirling herring gulls yelled and swooped on them. Mouse threw pebbles into the sea with a venom that told me he had not yet recovered his good humour after George's insults. I sent him off to the bakers to buy a bag of Danish pastries and chocolate croissants to give us a sugar boost later in the morning.

I crossed the threshold into the shop and noticed that the post had been picked up and placed in a neat pile on the counter. Only one person who worked in the shop had OCD.

'Amanda, is that you?' I said.

'I'm up here,' she said, leaning over the bannister.

'Thank goodness. Are you okay?'

'A little shocked, but I guess so.'

'I would be too. What are you doing here? Wouldn't it be sensible to take some time off after what happened yesterday?'

'I came to get some project documents as insurance for the future. I'm leaving the project immediately. I don't know where I'll be going, though. Probably back to my parents' house for now.'

'I'm sorry to hear that. You didn't deserve to get caught up in this horrible situation. Mouse will be devastated.'

'I'm going to miss him too, but I have no choice. Do you know what happened to the papers from my desk? Did the police take them too?'

'Mouse and I took them home to the Grotty Hovel last night to search for evidence that you didn't kill David. We showed George a photograph David took with his phone, and which you and Mouse included in the MPA presentation.'

'It was you who found the photograph? How did you know it came from David's phone?'

'I recognised it as one David showed to me on board the fishing boat.'

'I'm so grateful. The police raid yesterday really freaked me out. I couldn't believe it when they pulled the wig and dress out of my file drawer. I've never seen them before.'

'Mouse convinced me you had been framed. You should thank him for being freed.'

'I will. Can I collect the papers from your house? I want to go through the accounts and I don't have my computer yet. The police are copying the hard drive first.'

'Sure. Mouse is at the bakery. Why don't you walk there and he can open up for you? I'll mind the shop.'

Amanda came downstairs and gave me a brief hug before almost skipping down the road towards the bakery. Poor old Mouse would not be happy. He had formed an attachment to Amanda and would miss having someone with whom to go out on the town. At least they could text each other no matter where Amanda went, and I rather uncharitably reflected that ninety per cent of their relationship consisted of texting each other anyway. At least George had acted quickly on our evidence and released her. I crossed my fingers Roz and Ed would soon be free again too. There seemed no reason to hold them now Lexi had shown her hand.

Before I could do anything useful, Lexi arrived at the shop, full of the joys of spring.

'Isn't it a glorious morning?' she said, pushing her shades up onto her head. 'I'm not sure I feel like working at all today.'

I tried not to act surprised at her total lack of reaction to events, but the smug look on her face spurred me into wiping it straight off.

'Did you really think you could frame Amanda?' I said. 'The police will soon find out who loaded David's photographs onto your server. How are you going to explain that?'

Her face turned as white as a sheet, and she put out a hand to steady herself on the counter.

'How did you? Where? Oh my God.'

She sank into a chair and put her head in her hands. I did not move towards her. My lack of sympathy for her state made her raise it again, her face hard and unyielding.

'You don't know anything,' she said. 'Amanda is no angel. I found out she was blackmailing David.'

'About his real name? Or about causing your sister to kill herself?'

Lexi's eyes almost burst out of her head.

'How could you be so cruel? What have I ever done to you? There's a lot you don't understand. At least give me a chance to explain.'

A genuine sob escaped her throat, and I caved in a little. She would have to tell the police anyway, but George would not give me the details I could glean now.

'You deserve that much, I suppose. As Ghita would say, I think it's time for a cup of tea.'

Soon we were ensconced on the window seat with a large pot of Darjeeling brewing on the table in front of us and for once, a little milk jug and sugar bowl too. Lexi had refused cake, and mindful of the baked goods on their way to me, I did too.

'Why don't you start at the beginning?' I said.

'How much do you know?' said Lexi.

'David was a fraud who capitalised on his relationship with your sister to get accepted into upper-class circles and then dumped her, resulting in her suicide. How did you start working together?'

'He disappeared off the radar for years after Hazel died. I thought he had left the country. Then I heard someone needed a consultant to market their environmental projects. When it turned out to be David, I realised I had a chance for revenge. He had only ever seen me once, and he didn't recognise me. I thought I could expose him as a fraud and bankrupt him, take away his position in society. Unfortunately, I fell under his spell. Don't ask me what happened, but I became enthralled by his charm and passion. I found it hard to carry out my plan. But then we came here, and he started chasing Roz, right under my nose. It reignited the hatred I had for him. When I heard him say he planned to go out night fishing with Ed, I decided to kill him and dump the body at sea.'

'But how were you going to do that?'

'I'm not sure. My brains were scrambled with hate. I thought if I told Ed about David and Roz, he would help me.'

'But why did you put on the wig and the dress?'

'I hated Roz for taking David away from me. I wasn't thinking straight.'

'That's no excuse. And now you tried to frame Amanda too? I don't think I can find any sympathy for you. The police must do the rest.'

I tried to stand up, but Lexi grabbed my arm.

'You don't understand. It's true I dressed up as Roz and I went to the boat to kill David, but I couldn't find him. I climbed on board and saw fresh blood on the floor and I completely freaked out. I thought Ed had found out about Roz already and killed David himself.'

'So, when the police blamed Ed, you said nothing about being there?'

'What was the point in incriminating myself? I rushed away still wearing the wig and the dress, and that's when I made the mistake of passing by that restaurant with the CCTV camera.'

I sighed.

'You're expecting me to believe that you didn't kill David, because someone beat you to it.'

'It's the truth. I swear on my sister's life. I didn't kill him.'

'But who did?'

The shop bell clanged below us and Constable Brennan entered the shop with another young police officer I didn't recognise. George came in behind them, his face set in detective mode. The constables waited downstairs while he came to join us. Lexi tried to cower behind me, but I stepped out of the way.

'Alexandra Burlington-Smythe, I'm Detective Inspector George Carter and I'm here to arrest you on suspicion of murder. You do not have to say anything. But it may harm your defense if you do not mention when questioned, something which you later rely on in court. Anything you say may be given in evidence. Do you understand?'

Lexi nodded. She gave me a pleading glance, but I had no intention of supporting her then. It seemed to me she had lied and taken advantage of us all, and thrown Amanda to the wolves without a second thought. But I felt unsure of her guilt despite everything. Who would swear their innocence on their sister's life like that? I doubted even she was capable of it. As I watched her being taken away and bundled into the patrol car, I felt terribly sad and worn out, as if the joy had been sucked out of life. I had been so excited to rent out my office, but it had been a disaster from start to finish, and I still had those damn taxidermy fish. Their accusing eyes stared at me from every corner of the shop. How could I ever get rid of them?

Chapter 32

I shut up shop early and headed home under a cloud. Lexi's panicked expression as they took her away had imprinted itself on my memory and I couldn't shake it. Mouse had returned from his time with Amanda in a deep depression. She had confessed the truth about being blackmailed by David over the minor amounts missing from the accounts. As a former juvenile delinquent, he was in no position to judge, and his voice broke when he confirmed her impending departure. We were a sorry pair when we arrived at the Grotty Hovel to nurse our respective wounds. Even a tasty early supper of cheese toasties with caramelised onion chutney did not raise our spirits, and we sat on the sofa drinking cans of Magners and sulking.

I was about to give up and take to my bed to read when the doorbell rang. I rolled my eyes and Mouse rushed upstairs. We both assumed it would be George come to gloat over his arrest, but we were wrong. Flo stood on the pavement holding a plastic bag of Chinese takeaway, drops of rain shining in her bun under the streetlight. I beamed at her and she gave me a damp hug.

'How are my Grotty Hovelers?' she said. 'I thought you might like some updates.'

I felt like I had eaten all day without a break, but it would have been churlish to refuse Flo's kind offering. Mouse came back downstairs and, as with all teenage boys, acted as if he hadn't eaten for a month. We all sat in the kitchen and I watched while Flo and Mouse competed to eat the most. I was dying to interrogate her, but I felt it would be churlish to interrupt their enjoyment. I munched on a crunchy spring roll dipped in hoisin sauce and bided my time. Finally, Flo patted her tummy.

'Boy, I needed that. We have been hysterically busy today.'

'Anything to do with David de Frontenac's murder?' I said.

'David Foster? Well, I had the unpleasant task of asking his parents to identify his body when they haven't seen him for fifteen years and had already registered him as missing, possibly deceased.'

'Gosh, that's rough. I'm sorry. How did they take it?'

'Not well. His mother had hysterics and had to be given a tranquilliser. She told me she had always been sure he was still alive. Her husband just stood there with his mouth open. Everyone reacts differently to shock.'

'What did they make of his double life? It must have been awful for them to realise the life they made for him wasn't good enough,' said Mouse.

'I'm not sure they questioned his motives. His death hit them so hard,' said Flo.

'I'm sorry you had to cope with that. It must have been frightful,' I said.

'Horrendous. But I didn't come to tell you about that. We got the Murray's gun back from forensics.'

'That's great, or is it?' said Mouse.

'The news is good. Not only are the bullets completely different from the one recovered from David's body, but the gun has probably never been fired before.'

'That's wonderful. Did they release Ed?' I said.

'George cautioned him about wasting police time, but, yes, they did. And they sent the order to Bronzefield for the authorities to release Roz too. Ed went to the prison to pick her up this afternoon.'

Mouse clapped his hands together in delight, making Hades spit and sprint for the cat flap. I rolled my eyes. No one's trying to hurt you, Hades.

'Any news about Lexi's arrest?'

'We found some blonde hairs inside the skullcap of the curly wig, which I'm confident will match Lexi's hair, so Amanda's off the hook.'

'As if she would ever do something like that,' said Mouse.

'Also, Lexi confessed to being the person in the CCTV, but she swears there was nobody on the boat when she got there that night, only a patch of blood on the floor which was almost dry.'

'That's what she told me, but I found it hard to believe. If it's true, we've missed something vital,' I said.

'We need a summit to go over the timeline with everyone present,' said Mouse. 'We should get Ed and Roz and the rest of the gang to come to the Shanty tomorrow afternoon and use Ryan's white boards to work out who was where, and when.'

'Don't let George know what you're doing. He'll have a conniption,' said Flo. 'I think this case is giving him grey hairs.'

'He'll be blaming me, as usual,' I said.

'Inevitable, my dear Watson,' said Flo.

'I'll start rounding up the troops,' said Mouse, scrolling through his phone.

'Call Joy first and make sure they don't mind us using their pub for the summit. She needs to be at the meeting as she saw some of the comings and goings that night. It's essential we understand what times people left the pub and who she saw at the harbour.'

'Do you want Harry to come?' said Mouse.

'Of course. He found out about the Burgess connection, although I'm pretty sure Frank has been eliminated as a suspect ages ago.'

'Don't forget Len,' said Flo.

'He's a suspect. I'm not inviting him. It's getting more like a Poirot mystery all the time,' I said. 'I should get one of those fake waxed moustaches to wear.'

'I'm not inviting any suspects,' Mouse said. 'We won't announce the murderer, although we might realise who it is if we eliminate everyone else.'

'How will you know who is innocent and who is guilty? This case would be better left to the police,' said Flo.

I laughed.

'Now where's the fun in that?'

Chapter 33

Luckily, everyone could come to the Shanty the next afternoon. Joy agreed to set up a situation room in the bar and to provide refreshments. I don't understand how anyone can think clearly without a sugar boost. Mouse and I arrived early so we could set up the timeline on the boards with Joy. We left the Mini in the car park and traipsed through the wet grass to the cliff path muttering about the rubbish English summer. Harry caught up with us halfway to the pub and gave me a quick kiss when Mouse wasn't looking. He had not been around for a few days, but I think we both needed time to reflect after our moment at the Swedish clearance. Two steps forward, one back. It was like trying to walk through a minefield. His kiss made my lips buzz and my heart sing, but I tried to maintain my focus on the case. Mouse threw his arm around Harry's shoulders and they walked in lockstep together. I walked behind them, my heart full.

The interior of the Shanty felt different every time I stepped in through the low door. This time the whiteboards gave it the feel of an offsite training day. The informal setting gave lie to the serious purpose of the meeting, but the serious intent had not been totally camouflaged. I gave Joy a hug and inquired after Ryan.

'Prague, I'm afraid,' she said. 'He'll be spitting that he missed this. He loves a bit of intrigue.'

I smiled. And what did he do on those trips if it hadn't got something to do with intrigue? I doubted we would ever find out.

Harry and Mouse went over to the boards and drew out timelines and lists of clues and then removed them again. I left them to it and helped Joy make pots of coffee and put home baked shortbread onto plates. I helped myself to a piece, and its warm buttery taste made me lick my lips and crave more. If Ghita didn't start her Fat Fighters classes again soon, I would have to be wheeled around in a bath-chair. She had been absent from Second Home recently because of a mysterious project she had undertaken. I felt the absence of my two friends like holes in my heart. The thought of seeing Roz filled one hole with pure joy.

And I didn't have to wait for long. The loud sound of Roz's raucous laughter cut through the pub and seconds later she stomped inside in a cloud of blonde curls and diaphanous fabric. I rushed over and enveloped her in a hug. Ed held her hand like a drowning man and I stretched over to kiss his cheek. A fat tear escaped and ran down my face landing in a wet blob on my denim shirt. I didn't have time to recover or even ask them questions before Ghita burst in and grabbed both myself and Roz in a group embrace.

'Never let this happen again,' she said, and we didn't need to ask what she meant.

We had set this up as a Seacastle Mysteries committee meeting, and only residents were invited. After much

224

discussion, we had agreed not to invite anyone else connected to the case. Once everyone had got seated with their choice of hot beverage and a triangle of scrumptious shortbread, I tapped the whiteboard with a marker.

'Okay, let's start at the beginning. David de Frontenac's real name was David Foster, and he grew up in Hull where he did a degree in environmental sciences.'

I had forgotten how many of us didn't know that yet. Roz and Ed looked stunned. I waited for all the gasps and comments to die away.

'During that degree, he went out with a certain Hazel Smith. He took advantage of her contacts to get himself accepted in high society and to learn how to speak with received pronunciation.'

'No wonder he sounded like someone off the BBC,' said Ed.

'He dumped Hazel Smith just before the Leavers' Ball and she later killed herself. We have discovered that Hazel was Lexi's sister.'

Another round of gasps accompanied this revelation. I started to enjoy myself.

'When David changed his name to de Frontenac, he advertised for someone to help him navigate high society and market his environmental projects. Lexi came to the interview and recognised him immediately. He, on the other hand, did not, as they had only met briefly years before. Impressed by her skill set, he took her on. Lexi intended to get her revenge on him by exposing his sham background and ruining his reputation, but she became seduced by his charisma and fell in love with him instead.'

'Then they came to Seacastle?' said Ghita.

'Exactly. David did his usual thing and flirted with every woman he came across, but he met his match in Roz. He fell for her and she wouldn't have him. She doesn't mind flirting, but she loves Ed passionately.'

'With all my heart,' said Roz, and snuggled closer to Ed, who cleared his throat.

'On the day of the murder, we went diving in Ed's boat. On the way home, Ed fought with Len Graves about his involvement in the cigarette smuggling ring and threatened to shop him to the police.'

'If David hadn't made a pass at Roz, I might have killed Len instead. I mean. You know what I mean.'

'Unfortunate turn of phrase,' said Joy, but she smiled at him.

'Anyway, Ed told David to lay off Roz, or he'd kill him.'

'Another faux pas,' said Joy. 'Perfect fodder for P.C. Plod.'

'Anyway, when we got to shore, I left with Harry, because I wanted to get home and out of my wet clothes. Bert set off for a pint at the Shanty and David promised to join him later before he set sail with Ed. So, Ed stays on the boat and gets ready to set sail—'

'No, I didn't. I went to buy some provisions in Shoreham and I didn't return for several hours,' said Ed.

'I got to the boat before Ed did,' said Roz. 'I had planned to surprise him.'

'What time was that?' I said.

'About nine o'clock. That's when I found the cigarettes hidden in the bulkhead. Len must have put them there before I arrived. I used a fish trolley to take them to a beach hut.'

Mouse added this to the timeline and nodded at me.

'Joy knows what happened next,' I said.

'Bert Higgins and David were drinking together with some of the other fishermen. Bert stayed in the pub all evening, but David left when Len arrived just before ten o'clock,' said Joy.

'That means David bumped into Roz not long after ten pm at the beach huts, and he had tripped over a lobster pot just before Ed walked by,' I said.

'I found a distressed Roz beside David, who had passed out, so I sent her home and said I would deal with it. David had obviously had a lot to drink. He stood up and insisted he was okay, but his top was soaking wet. I gave him mine and told him to go to the boat and wait for me while I went home to get another,' said Ed.

'What time was that?' said Mouse.

'Ten thirty,' said Ed. 'I checked my watch because I didn't want to miss the tide, but I decided it wouldn't make much difference if I left a little later.'

'Ed got home not long after me,' said Roz. 'I heard him make a cup of coffee and digging in the trunk for something. Later, I worried he had taken the gun from there, so I pretended he hadn't come home. But now I know he just took another hoody and a rain jacket for David. When I heard him leave, I fell asleep.'

'Let me get this straight,' said Harry. 'David walked to the boat at about ten thirty with Ed's hoody on. That means he was murdered between then and eleven fifteen pm when Ed got back to the boat and left the harbour.'

'But that leaves Ed in the frame,' said Roz.

'Not really. Your gun was never fired and the bullets are different. Unless Ed bought a gun in Shoreham,' I said.

Ed rolled his eyes.

'I don't think they sell World War two pistols in Sainsburys,' he said.

'We know Lexi got to the boat just before it sailed, so she must have been there after the murderer and before Ed, unless she's the murderer,' I said.

'She's certainly up there in pole position,' said Mouse. 'According to the time line there's a twenty-minute window for the murder.'

'She swore on the life of her sister that she didn't kill him, and despite my dislike of the way she has behaved, I believed her,' I said. 'There's something we're missing.'

'What about the second phone call?' said Harry. 'Didn't you say Pat Grady claimed to receive another phone call from the payphone that night?'

The cogs in my head whirred, and the truth broke through the fog as I added up the clues.

'He did. He also claimed to have seen Ed going to the boat at ten o'clock,' I said. 'But what if it was David?'

'What time did he receive the second call?' said Roz.

'An hour after the first call,' I said, my heart rate rising. 'That would be ten forty-five.'

'And how did somebody know about the murder before it happened?' said Ed.

We all looked at each other in astonishment as the penny dropped.

'What do you mean?' said Mouse.

I remembered Grady telling me about the phone call, and I nodded my head.

'You're right,' I said. 'If the call was made from the phone box, that means the murder had to take place approximately twenty minutes earlier, in order to give someone time to drive to the phone. Theoretically, that means the murder took place at ten-twenty-five.'

'But David hadn't walked to the boat before ten thirty,' said Ed. 'So why did Pat Grady lie about the second call?'

'Oh my heavens,' said Roz. 'I should have guessed. Pat has had a crush on me forever. He's always been resentful of our marriage. He thought Ed cheated him out of marrying me. I would rather die than let Pat Grady anywhere near me, but maybe he tried to get rid of Ed to give him a chance.'

'You mean he killed David by mistake because he had my hoody on?' said Ed. 'That makes sense. It's pitch dark in that cabin with no lights on. Maybe David hadn't found the light switch yet. He was pretty drunk. If Pat realised he had killed the wrong man, he could have shoved him in the bulkhead. Then he may have heard Lexi turn up and hidden in the shadows. When I got on board about five minutes later, and David wasn't there, I thought he had changed his mind about coming with me and gone home. I didn't notice the blood on the floor. I guess it had dried by then. I didn't want to miss the tide, so I set out to sea immediately.'

'So, since Len had already called about contraband on your boat, Pat realised he could frame you for David's murder. He must have been ecstatic.'

'Why did he invent the second call?'

'To confuse the police. He must have realised they were closing in. He thought he would give himself a better alibi if he were answering a call while the murder took place. But he over-elaborated.' I said. 'George says that's common in guilty people.'

'I can't believe it. He's so anonymous,' said Roz.

'A man with a grudge is capable of anything,' said Harry.

'Jealousy is one of the main motives for murder,' I said. 'I'd better let George know what we've figured out. He can check on the calls to the coastguard. I'm willing to bet there wasn't a second call made that night after all. This exonerates Lexi too. She doesn't appear on CCTV until after the fake phone call. The police should raid Grady's house and pick him up before he realises the game is up.'

'I expect they'll find the gun there too,' said Harry.

'Who needs a drink?' said Joy.

Chapter 34

What with celebrating Roz and Ed's release from prison, and our brilliance as detectives, we didn't leave the Shanty until closing time. We were all the worse for wear, and since we had all been drinking, even Ghita, nobody could drive home. Mouse dug up a minivan and driver from Uber who waited for us all in the car park and drove around Seacastle, depositing everyone at their houses. Harry stayed with us on the sofa at the Grotty Hovel. I think he fell asleep before his head hit the cushions of the sofa. Hades soon found him and curled up near his head, purring like a Maserati engine. He's such a tart!

I resisted the temptation to call George, as I am not a fan of the drunken call trope, and I worried he might bring up his proposal again. I had no intention of accepting, but I couldn't help gloating over the position he found himself in because of his own stupid decisions. Sharon was welcome to him. Harry and I needed the chance to try out our rising libidos with nobody watching. I felt like a teenager debating with herself over losing her virginity when I imagined going to bed with him. The excitement of the planning worried me in case the real thing didn't come up to scratch for one of us. Middle-aged dating is not for sissies.

I called George as soon as I woke up, which was close to midday, wincing as he bellowed down the line at me, his usual volume. He put his hand over the receiver to relay instructions to his team, but I could still hear him shouting instructions about getting a warrant to check the calls to the coastguard.

'This is a genuine breakthrough,' he said when he got back on the line. 'I'm grateful. The Super has been breathing down my neck this week at our lack of progress and Lexi has refused to eat for two days.'

'Will you release her now?' I said.

'I don't see any point in keeping her here. Where would she have got a gun from anyway?'

I decided not to tell him about Lexi's father. I didn't want to complicate matters. Lexi's father who had my taxidermy fish I reminded myself and sighed.

'I don't know why you're sighing,' said George. 'I'm the one that's got to arrest someone with a gun who has already shown he's prepared to use it.'

'Be careful,' I said.

George grunted and hung up. I turned to see Harry standing beside me.

'Your hair looks like a bird's nest,' he said.

'And yours resembles a bare arse, but I know which I'd prefer.'

He laughed.

'Are you hungry? We could eat a Chinese down at the harbour.'

'A Chinese? Isn't it a bit early for lunch?'

'By the time we get down there, it will be half past twelve.'

'What about Mouse?' I said.

'Still dead to the world. We can bring him a takeaway.'

'What about my shop?'

'It doesn't eat Chinese. Brush your hair and let's go.'

We sauntered along the promenade and down the hill to the harbour past the beach huts before turning into the side street that held Mr Chen's restaurant. I could already feel saliva in my mouth in anticipation of some sweet and sour chicken and fried rice. Mr Chen's face lit up when we arrived and he directed us to the small window table. Harry ordered beef with mushrooms and bamboo shoots. We both ordered a Fanta Lemon, which made me smile as everyone else I knew drank Coke or Pepsi. As usual, the food tasted delicious, and I ate far too much. We bought a helping of shredded roast duck with hoisin sauce for Mouse and staggered out onto the street.

'I'm too full to go home yet,' I said. 'Do you mind if we go for a walk along the harbour pier before we head for home?'

'Not at all. Lead on.'

We linked arms and strolled along, inspecting the lobster pots and the stacks of nets and buoys. The tide had gone out, and we walked down to the small beach to poke about in the rock pools. I found an upturned starfish which I righted and watched it mine its way under the sand with its hundreds of creamy cilia. I straightened up and strolled over to Harry who was inspecting a stack of fish crates.

Suddenly, a man stepped out from behind them and pointed a gun at me. Pat Grady. The police raid must have gone wrong somehow. I froze and the food I had eaten felt like a granite weight in my stomach. Pat grabbed my arm and tugged me to his side. He smelled like he hadn't bathed for days. The foul mix of sweat and alcohol made me flinch.

'You're coming with me,' he said, his grip tightening as I pulled against it.

Harry turned towards the voice, and the smile faded from his face. His demeanour changed in an instant, and a dangerous quiet overtook him. I had seen him like this before. I put up my hand, but he stood between Pat and the mainland, his body stiff like a mastiff's.

'Put down the gun,' he said.

'I don't think so,' said Pat. 'I'm taking her with me.'

'You'll have to go through me first.'

I tried to say something, but my throat wouldn't respond. Pat's upper lip lifted into a sneer.

'You think I won't shoot?' he said. 'I already killed that nancy boy on the boat. Do you really think I won't kill you too?'

'I think you're making a big mistake. Put down the gun.'

Harry's face resembled a granite cliff, giving nothing away. A herring gull flew overhead, screeching ownership of some fish scraps being offloaded on the beach. Time stood still. Grady raised the gun, and before I could react, he fired at Harry. I screamed in pain as a sharp retort hurt my ear. I had the vague sensation that both Harry and Pat had gone down. Harry lay at my feet, his hands stretched towards me. He rolled onto his back and sat up, groaning.

'Remind me not to eat so much next time,' he said. 'I couldn't get off the ground.'

He stood up and bent over Pat Grady who clutched his hand, moaning in pain. It bled profusely, leaving a red pool on the paving. I stared at it in shock. I couldn't understand what had happened.

'Get up,' said Harry. 'Leave the gun on the ground.'

His tone brooked no refusal. Grady tottered to his feet. The gun lay on the pier, its barrel shattered. A smell of cordite drifted on the wind. Loud footsteps approached. George and Constable Brennan appeared puffing and panting with an armed officer. George took in the scene and directed P.C. Brennan to read Grady his rights. He then gave me a hug, muttering in my ear, 'thank goodness you're all right.' Harry stood to one side, bemused. I freed myself and went to Harry's side.

'Harry saved my life,' I said. 'He faced Grady down.'

'What happened?' said George.

'He took a pot shot at me, but the gun misfired,' said Harry.

'A streak of luck,' said George.

'Not really,' said Harry. 'The Enfield number two revolver has always been a liability. I was issued one of those as a personal protection weapon when I worked with the UDR in Belfast for two weeks. They issued six rounds of fifty-year-old ammo to me. Before handing it back to the armoury, I fired the six rounds for a lark with a friend: two were misfires, two rounds ejected the bullets a small distance, one fired correctly and the other round lodged in the barrel. As I told you, Enfield revolvers were famous for being worse than useless. I took a chance Grady's weapon would be similarly crap.'

'Russian roulette,' said George. 'Remind me not to play chicken with you. We'll take Grady to the station if you two are okay. Can you stick around until forensics arrives so nobody touches the fragments?'

'We'll be fine,' I said, and Harry nodded.

I noticed he had turned as pale as snow, and I made him sit down on a bench nearby. George left with his prisoner and the other officers, looking behind him and shaking his head. I put my hand on Harry's shoulder and he jumped.

'Are you okay?' I said.

'I'll be fine. Give me a few minutes to get my head straight.'

I took his hand and felt him trembling. I sat beside him and pulled his head to my chest. He hid his face from me and his shoulders heaved as he struggled to retake control. I waited quietly until he pulled himself upright again.

'You saved my life, you complete idiot,' I said.

'Not on purpose.'

'I love you, Harry Fletcher.'

He looked me straight in the eye and said, 'No, you don't. You're just suffering from shock.'

I nodded, deadpan.

'That must be it.'

Was I disappointed he didn't say it too? No. I loved him. I knew he loved me too. It wasn't so much a declaration as an affirmation of something we both already knew. I looked forward to saying it again in a more tender moment with all the meaning imbued in the phrase when uttered by a lover. I also knew at that moment that George was toast, no matter how much he wanted to get back with me. It would never happen. I think he knew it too from the look he gave me as he walked away with Grady and saw us together on the bench.

George called us later in the afternoon and asked us to make statements for the investigation while the incident stayed fresh in our memories. We went to the station and were both questioned as witnesses. I found it peculiar to be back at the station again after such a short period. P.C. Brennan took my statement and George took Harry's. We left the station together. Harry looked at his phone.

'Hey, guess what? I've got a clearance tomorrow. Fancy a day trip?'

'Are you kidding? Of course. I'm desperate to get out of here after everything that's happened.'

'Okay. I'll pick you up at ten o'clock at the Grotty Hovel. I've got to sort out some stuff. I'll see you tomorrow.'

And with that, he left me standing outside the station. I felt abandoned by his abrupt departure, after all we'd been through, but I tried not to take it personally. We were going on a clearance, weren't we? He'd hardly abandoned me. I shook myself and strode towards the Second Home where I found a couple outside staring in at one of my taxidermy fish.

'Can I help you?' I said, crossing my fingers I had finally found a buyer. 'I'm the owner of Second Home.'

'Did you catch that fish?' said the man.

'Um, no. It's Victorian. About 100 years old.'

'How do you know?' said his wife.

'How do I know what?'

'The age of the fish. Can you tell by its teeth?'

I looked from him to his wife and back and decided he had never told a joke in his life.

'Yes,' I said.

'I told you so,' said the man, walking away with his wife.

I unlocked the door and stepped inside. The rest of the fish stared at me from their perches with their goggly eyes. I decided I didn't need to open the shop for a day or two, so I went outside again and locked the door before walking home.

Chapter 35

The next morning, I showered and put on fresh clothes ready for the clearance with Harry. I fed Hades and left a note for Mouse with a twenty-pound note attached, asking him to take the day off and fend for himself. I felt so much lighter without the weight of the investigation hanging over me. I had saved my friends from prison, but Harry had almost died. Sticking to vintage sales and avoiding complex murder cases seemed like an excellent idea to me.

On the bright side, Seacastle Council was close to agreement on granting Marine Protection Area status for the kelp sanctuary. Before his death, David had worked his magic on all the female stakeholders except Marion Pocock, but Ghita had let her know we were aware of her kinship with Frank Burgess and her bluster had deflated somewhat. The fishermen were resigned to their fate and Lexi had put them in contact with the Lyme Bay association who ran the MPA in the bay. They had both positive and negative stories to tell about their protected area, but Ed and his friends hoped to glean information on how to profit from the sanctuary.

I made a flask of tea and some ham sandwiches and put them in a bag with a selection of fruit on the turn, which needed to be finished up. Harry would turn up at ten on the dot. His military background had made him punctual to a fault. My more lackadaisical approach to appointments did not go down well with him. He could be guaranteed to use his horn if I did not emerge from my door at precisely ten o'clock. I decided to surprise him. I stood outside the door with the picnic at five minutes to ten, intending to point at my watch when he arrived and make a show of him arriving late. The idea made me grin as I stepped outside and bumped into George who had his hand up to knock on the door.

'Hi,' he said. 'I was just coming to see you.'

'Hello George. What's up? Got any murders you want me to solve?'

He frowned.

'No.'

'What are you doing here, then?' I said.

'I, um, I hoped we might go for a drive,' he said.

I blinked.

'What? Oh. No. I can't. I've got a clearance. Harry should be here any minute.'

'Harry again. Is there something I should know?'

'We're divorced. There is nothing you should know about my life. Not anymore.'

'But we made a mistake. I want to discuss us getting remarried.'

I pinched myself to see if I was having a weird nightmare, but it felt genuine enough. George had an odd look on his face. I realised he expected me to react with joy and leap into his arms. He had them open in anticipation. I couldn't believe it. I shook my head at him and pushed him away.

'There is nothing to discuss. You live with Sharon. You need to work it out with her now.'

George's brow furrowed in confusion.

'But she's not the one. You are.'

Harry's van appeared at the top of the road.

'But you're not the one for me. I'm going out with Harry now.'

'Harry? Why didn't you tell me?'

'Because it's none of your business. I'm sorry. I've got to go now.'

Harry pulled up beside us and waited. I could see his fingers drumming on the steering wheel.

'I won't give up,' said George. 'I'll win you back.'

'Bye George,' I said, getting into the van and muttering 'drive' under my breath.

Harry took one look at my face and put his foot down. George stepped onto the road and watched the van all the way to the corner. The last glimpse I had of him; he had his hands on his hips. I could imagine his confusion. I had looked forward to this day for months, but now I couldn't imagine a worse idea.

'What's up?' said Harry. 'More murders?'

'Not yet. But if George keeps turning up at my house uninvited, I can think of one that's likely to happen.'

'Do you want to stay and talk to him?'

'Are you joking? I want to go with you and do a mahoosive clearance, not stay here with grumpy drawers.'

'Let's go then.'

It took almost an hour before the tight feeling in my chest released and I retrieved that road trip feeling. Harry let me process my thoughts without speaking. When I blew out a long breath, he patted me on the leg.

'Okay?'

'Yes. I'm sorry. George is having a mid-life crisis.'

'Didn't he have one of those already?'

'Yes, but now he's repenting or doubling down. I can't tell which. He wants to go back in time and try again.'

'With you?'

I nodded. Harry whistled.

'Whoa. That's heavy. Do you want George back?'

'No. I used to think I did, but I found something better.'

'Will he accept your decision?'

'Does he have a choice?'

Harry did not answer. His jaw muscle tightened as he digested our conversation.

'Am I the something you found?' he said finally.

I swallowed and panicked. I could feel his gaze on me as I pretended to be fascinated by the dashboard. Wiping imaginary dust from the dials with a tissue, I reddened under his scrutiny.

'Where's this house then?' I said, peering out of the window. 'Shouldn't we have arrived by now?'

'Stop avoiding the subject.'

'I'm not. Seriously, I think we drove past again.'

Harry's brow wrinkled. He pulled in to the side of the road and checked the GPS coordinates.

'We should be close,' he said. 'I reckon it's down one of these tiny lanes. Sometimes they're missing from the GPS.'

'Have you got a paper map?' I said.

'Nope. We will have to drive around and hope for the best.'

He turned the van around and pointed it down a small lane which did not look promising. It forked in two after a short way, and we took the lane on the left. There seemed to be a turning every few hundred yards and soon we were hopelessly lost. We drove around the maze of laneways for about half an hour until we came to a tiny village green with a bowling lawn shaded by a massive oak.

'Did you notice what the village is called?' said Harry.

'I'm afraid not. But there's a pub over there. Why don't we have a pit stop for coffee and ask the locals about this house?'

'Excellent plan. And maybe you can tell me about your choices?'

I sighed. As a newly graduated commitment-phobe, I did not feel ready to expose myself to scrutiny, even by someone I already loved. I couldn't tell you why I didn't want to fall straight into his arms. It's complicated.

The Fletcher's Arms, or my very own pub as Harry called it, typified the quintessential village meeting place. It had the typical timber frame of early coaching inns, and wonky windows in thick walls. The interior had an equine theme with collars and traces and harnesses draped on the beams and paintings of horses pulling mail coaches and Hansom cabs in different settings.

'What this pub needs is a taxidermy fish,' said Harry, making me crease with laughter.

The barman smirked.

'What'll it be, folks?' he said.

'We're looking for a house,' said Harry, checking his mobile phone. 'Harringale Hall?'

'I'm sorry. I've never heard of it, but I'm not from around here. If you wait for some regulars to come in, they'll be able to help you. Can I get you anything?'

'I'd love a coffee please, a latte if that's possible,' I said.

'Same for me,' said Harry, looking around the pub. 'Hey, there's a darts board. Can you throw a decent dart?'

'I can, as it happens,' I said.

I wondered if I should warn him I used to play in a league, but he didn't ask…

'There's a set behind the bar if you'd like to play,' said the barman.

'Magic,' said Harry. 'Get in the coffees and we'll start the game now.'

He handed me the darts, and I popped open the plastic case. The dart flights were feather, and the barrels made of brass. Nice old-fashioned darts. My favourite. I weighed one in my hand.

'Scared?' said Harry.

'You wish.'

I strode to the mat and lined up the board.

'Do you know how cute you look when you stick the tip of your tongue out?'

'Are you trying to put me off?'

'Not much.'

I threw three darts. The first bounced off the outer ring, the second in the no. 1 segment, and the third in triple twenty. Harry's expression went from grinning to astonished.

'Were you aiming for a triple top?' he said.

'Was I supposed to aim for something else?' I said, trying to appear innocent.

Harry roared with laughter.

'Oh my days. We have a ringer. I don't Adam and Eve it.'

'Do you surrender?'

'Don't be silly. This is going to be fun.'

And it was. The day wore on. No one had heard of Harringale Hall, or if they had, they didn't know where it was. We ate steak and kidney pies with baked potatoes for lunch and played darts for hours. The coffees got exchanged for drinks and all hope of leaving the pub went up in smoke. As the evening drew in, we sat in the snug and talked about George and Cathy and us without barriers. I felt my heart melting and fusing over the damage done by my divorce. There was never any discussion about going home. The pub had rooms, and we booked one after a couple of drinks. Only one. We were way past pretending at that stage.

Chapter 36

The shop almost echoed with emptiness after the project office had been shut down. I had grown used to Mouse and Amanda giggling together, and Lexi's bawdy reminiscences about media parties I missed. The glass floats spun in the sea breeze that invaded the ground floor as I entered and blew the cobwebs from the lamps hanging from the ceiling. I trod on some post which had been shoved through the letterbox and left a boot mark on the envelopes. I went through them, throwing the junk mail straight into the dustbin and putting the bills to one side. I could not imagine how I would pay them and my heart sank. Maybe Harry would magic up another road trip for us, although he had sulked terribly after the last one. Despite me assuring him I didn't mind about his drink-fuelled malfunction; he took it hard. I knew he'd get over himself eventually.

Harry was not the only one sulking. George had not followed up on his threat to fight for me. Perhaps Sharon got wind of his unhappiness and had paid him a little more attention. She couldn't afford to lose her meal ticket as she had lost her job. As far as I was concerned, they deserved each other.

Then I noticed an old-fashioned, lavender, handwritten envelope (Basildon Bond!) with a local stamp on it among the bills. I turned it over twice and even sniffed it. Almost nobody wrote letters anymore, except for my sister, and she did it to show other people up. She sent out a constant stream of thank you notelets with flowery covers, condolence letters, yearly updates on the life of her children and her dog, and her husband's achievements at work. Poor henpecked Martin. But I could recognise her childish writing with its rounded letters, and this determined scrawl did not originate from her pen. I took the letter upstairs with me and made myself a latte, adding a sneaky spoon of sugar to lift my spirits.

When I had settled into the window seat, I slid a knife under the seal and opened the letter. Inside, I found a folded piece of lavender paper with several neat paragraphs written on it. A cheque floated to the floor, and I scrabbled under the table, trying to pick it up. Once I had righted myself again, I examined the cheque. Seven hundred and fifty pounds! That should pay all my bills. I couldn't read the signature, so I unfolded the letter and checked the sender's name. To my amazement, it had been sent by Lexi. She must have written it before she left for France. I wondered who had posted it for her. Probably Sally Wright at reception. She had been kind to Roz and Lexi and I didn't plan on forgetting that. Also, she had proven herself a discreet source of information when George had shut the spigot; surely someone to be cultivated.

I read the military lines of writing with some trepidation, but I soon relaxed. The style sounded like Lexi talking with plenty of exclamation marks and exaggeration. She did not mention the sanctuary or David, but asked me how the shop was doing and whether Roz and Ed had made up yet. She apologised for the delay in payment for her taxidermy fish and hoped I would forgive her.

'Whatever else I am, I'm not a thief.'

I felt a pang of sadness for her. She had been so keen on revenging herself against David, she almost ruined her own life instead. Luckily, the upper classes look after their own, and some rich pal had offered her a sojourn in the Dordogne to forget about her troubles and get relaunched.

David had paid a high price for his duplicity and philandering, but in the end, it hadn't affected the outcome. The sanctuary had been voted through despite the opposition of Frank Burgess, who didn't know when he was beaten. Even Marion Pocock has voted in favour, although I suspect Ghita has something to do with that. The fishermen had unanimously voted in favour of the sanctuary after a meeting they had at Lyme Bay with their fishing brethren who had already witnessed a large increase in biodiversity since imposing a near-shore Marine Protection area, which prohibited bottom trawling. Roz told me Ed had bought lobster pots and other static gear to trap more valuable seafood and he intended to diversify his offering to the fishmongers and restaurants. Their marriage had been strengthened by the near-affair with David. Roz would still crave attention and Ed would still get jealous, but they knew who they could count on in stormy seas.

At least Mouse seemed settled. He had missed Amanda a lot when she first left, but they had since bought tickets to Glastonbury so their relationship seemed to be intact. Only Hades had a free ticket to a quiet life; free food, accommodation and cuddles on tap. Sometimes I wished we could swap places.

The doorbell jangled as Ghita pushed it open. Behind her were two men, one of whom I recognised with a start as Rohan, her abortive match from Brighton. The other man, a short, stocky blond, carried a man-bag and stood with his hands on his hips like a handsome teapot. I bounced down the stairs to welcome them. Ghita had an enormous smile on her face. She pointed at the two men.

'Hi Tanya,' she said. 'You remember Rohan? And this is his partner, Kieron.'

'You came,' I said. 'How wonderful to see you. And to meet Kieron. Who wants cake and coffee?'

'I'll have a double espresso,' said Kieron. 'Is it okay if I take a poke about?'

'He likes a poke,' said Rohan, smirking.

'Naughty,' said Kieron and disappeared into the back, oohing and aahing.

Ghita and Rohan followed me upstairs, and I cut us all a piece of carrot cake while Ghita made herself a tea and Rohan an Americano. I still had some latte in my cup and I refreshed it with a shot of espresso. I noticed that Ghita and Rohan were holding hands, which confused me no end. However, seeing her happy made everything all right.

'So, what brings you to the bright Metropolis of Seacastle?' I said.

Before Rohan could formulate an answer, Ghita blurted out an explanation.

'He's moving here. Well, they both are. Brighton's too expensive and Kieron's a chef and they want to open a restaurant and I said why didn't they come here and they said they would have a look and…'

Ghita paused to take a breath. I grinned at Rohan.

'You're moving here? How wonderful. I hope we'll be seeing a lot of you.'

'I expect so. Ghita's agreed to help us get set up. She's an amazing cook, so Kieron is hoping they can imagine up some exquisite fusion recipes for our menu.'

Ghita blushed and giggled. Kieron's head appeared above the bannister and it swivelled around.

'Oh, my goodness,' he said. 'I can't believe it. There are more of them.'

'More of what, sweetness?' said Rohan.

'The fish. Haven't you seen them? I can't quite believe it. They are absolutely perfect for decorating our restaurant. They are for sale, aren't they?'

I nodded and crossed my fingers under the table.

'Most definitely. They're not cheap though.'

'Cheap, sneap,' said Rohan. 'Can we do them as a job lot?'

I beamed.

'I'm sure we can come to some arrangement.'

I hope you have enjoyed Eternal Forest. I would very much appreciate you leaving a review. It doesn't have to be a thesis. A couple of lines would be great. It helps me to sell more books. Thank you.

The next book in the series is Fatal Tribute. You can order the eBook now, by scanning this QR code with your phone, or go direct to PJ Skinner on Amazon:

You can buy all my books in paperback direct from my website. Use this QR code to get there.

Other Books in the Seacastle Series

Deadly Return (Book 1)

What if proving a friend's husband innocent of murder implicates her instead?

Tanya Bowe, an ex-investigative journalist, and divorcee, runs a vintage shop in the coastal town of Seacastle. When her old friend, Lexi Burlington-Smythe borrows the office above the shop as a base for the campaign to create a kelp sanctuary off the coast, Tanya is thrilled with the chance to get involved and make some extra money. Tanya soon gets drawn into the high-stake arguments surrounding the campaign, as tempers are frayed, and her friends, Roz and Ghita favour opposing camps. When a celebrity eco warrior is murdered, the evidence implicates Roz's husband Ed, and Tanya finds her loyalties stretched to breaking point as she struggles to discover the true identity of the murderer.

Fatal Tribute (Book 3)

How do you find the murderer, when every act is convincing?

Tanya Bowe, an ex-investigative journalist, agrees to interview the contestants of the National Talent Competition for the local newspaper, but finds herself up to her neck in secrets, sabotage and simmering resentment. The tensions increase when her condescending sister comes to stay next door for the duration of the contest.

Hunter Dorman, the rising star on the circuit is tipped to win the competition, but old stager, Lance Emerald, is not going down without a fight. When Lance is found dead in his dressing room, Tanya is determined to find the murderer but complex dynamics between the contestants and fraught family relationships make the mystery harder to solve. Can Tanya uncover the truth before another murder takes centre stage?

Other books by the Author

I write under various pen names in different genres. If you are looking for another mystery, why don't you try **Mortal Mission,** written as Pip Skinner.

Mortal Mission

Will they find life on Mars, or death?

When the science officer for the first crewed mission to Mars dies suddenly, backup Hattie Fredericks gets the coveted place on the crew. But her presence on the Starship provokes suspicion when it coincides with a series of incidents which threaten to derail the mission.

After a near-miss while landing on the planet, the world watches as Hattie and her fellow astronauts struggle to survive. But, worse than the harsh elements on Mars, is their growing realisation that someone, somewhere, is trying to destroy the mission.

When more astronauts die, Hattie doesn't know who to trust. And her only allies are 35 million miles away. As the tension ratchets up, violence and suspicion invade both worlds. If you like science-based sci-fi and a locked-room mystery with a twist, you'll love this book.

The Green Family Saga (written as Kate Foley) – a family saga set in Ireland

Rebel Green – Book 1

Relationships fracture when two families find themselves caught up in the Irish Troubles.

The Green family move to Kilkenny from England in 1969, at the beginning of the conflict in Northern Ireland. They rent a farmhouse on the outskirts of town, and make friends with the O'Connor family next door. Not every member of the family adapts easily to their new life, and their differing approaches lead to misunderstandings and friction. Despite this, the bonds between the family members deepen with time.

Perturbed by the worsening violence in the North threatening to invade their lives, the children make a pact never to let the troubles come between them. But promises can be broken, with tragic consequences for everyone.

Africa Green – Book 2

Will a white chimp save its rescuers or get them killed?

Journalist Isabella Green travels to Sierra Leone, a country emerging from civil war, to write an article about a chimp sanctuary. Animals that need saving are her obsession, and she can't resist getting involved with the project, which is on the verge of bankruptcy. She forms a bond with local boy, Ten, and army veteran, Pete, to try and save it. When they rescue a rare white chimp from a village frequented by a dangerous rebel splinter group, the resulting media interest could save the sanctuary.

But the rebel group have not signed the cease fire. They believe the voodoo power of the white chimp protects them from bullets, and they are determined to take it back so they can storm the capital. When Pete and Ten go missing, only Isabella stands in the rebels' way. Her love for the chimps unlocks the fighting spirit within her. Can she save the sanctuary or will she die trying?

Fighting Green – Book 3

Liz Green is desperate for a change. The Dot-Com boom is raging in the City of London, and she feels exhausted and out of her depth. Added to that, her long-term boyfriend, Sean O'Connor, is drinking too much and shows signs of going off the rails. Determined to start anew, Liz abandons both Sean and her job, and buys a near-derelict house in Ireland to renovate. She moves to Thomastown where she renews old ties and makes new ones, including two lawyers who become rivals for her affection. When Sean's attempt to win her back goes disastrously wrong, Liz finishes with him for good. Finding herself almost penniless, and forced to seek new ways to survive, Liz is torn between making a fresh start and going back to her old loves.

Can Liz make a go of her new life, or will her past become her future?

The Sam Harris Adventure Series

(written as PJ Skinner)

Set in the late 1980's and through the 1990's, this thrilling series follows the career of a female geologist. The first book sets the scene for the career of an unwilling heroine, whose bravery and resourcefulness are needed to navigate a series of adventures set in remote sites in Africa and South America. Based loosely on the real-life adventures of the author, the settings and characters are given an authenticity that will connect with readers who enjoy adventure fiction and thrillers set in remote settings with realistic scenarios. Themes such as women working in formerly male domains, and what constitutes a normal existence, are developed in the context of Sam's constant ability to find herself up to her neck in trouble. Sam's home life provides a contrast to her adventures and feeds her need to escape. Her attachment to an unfaithful boyfriend is the thread running through her romantic life, and her attempts to break free of it provide another side to her character.

Fool's Gold - Book 1

Newly qualified geologist Sam Harris is a woman in a man's world - overlooked, underpaid but resilient and passionate. Desperate for her first job, and nursing a broken heart, she accepts an offer from notorious entrepreneur Mike Morton, to search for gold deposits in the remote rainforests of Sierramar. With the help of nutty local heiress, Gloria Sanchez, she soon settles into life in Calderon, the capital. But when she accidentally uncovers a long-lost clue to a treasure buried deep within the jungle, her journey really begins. Teaming up with geologist Wilson Ortega, historian Alfredo Vargas and the mysterious Don Moises, they venture through the jungle, where she lurches between excitement and insecurity. Yet there is a far graver threat looming; Mike and Gloria discover that one of the members of the expedition is plotting to seize the fortune for himself and is willing to do anything to get it. Can Sam survive and find the treasure or will her first adventure be her last?

Hitler's Finger - Book 2

The second book in the Sam Harris Series sees the return of our heroine Sam Harris to Sierramar to help her friend Gloria track down her boyfriend, the historian, Alfredo Vargas. Geologist Sam Harris loves getting her hands dirty. So, when she learns that her friend Alfredo has gone missing in Sierramar, she gives her personal life some much needed space and hops on the next plane. But she never expected to be following the trail of a devious Nazi plot nearly 50 years after World War II … Deep in a remote mountain settlement, Sam must uncover the village's dark history. If she fails to reach her friend in time, the Nazi survivors will ensure Alfredo's permanent silence. Can Sam blow the lid on the conspiracy before the Third Reich makes a devastating return?

The background to the book is the presence of Nazi war criminals in South America which was often ignored by locals who had fascist sympathies during World War II. Themes such as tacit acceptance of fascism, and local collaboration with fugitives from justice are examined and developed in the context of Sam's constant ability to find herself in the middle of an adventure or mystery.

The Star of Simbako - Book 3

A fabled diamond, a jealous voodoo priestess, disturbing cultural practices. What could possibly go wrong? The third book in the Sam Harris Series sees Sam Harris on her first contract to West Africa to Simbako, a land of tribal kingdoms and voodoo. Nursing a broken heart, Sam Harris goes to Simbako to work in the diamond fields of Fona. She is soon involved with a cast of characters who are starring in their own soap opera, a dangerous mix of superstition, cultural practices, and ignorance (mostly her own). Add a love triangle and a jealous woman who wants her dead and Sam is in trouble again. Where is the Star of Simbako? Is Sam going to survive the chaos?

This book is based on visits made to the Paramount Chiefdoms of West Africa. Despite being nominally Christian communities, Voodoo practices are still part of daily life out there. This often leads to conflicts of interest. Combine this with the horrific ritual of FGM and it makes for a potent cocktail of conflicting loyalties. Sam is pulled into this life by her friend, Adanna, and soon finds herself involved in goings on that she doesn't understand.

The Pink Elephants - Book 4

Sam gets a call in the middle of the night that takes her to the Masaibu project in Lumbono, Africa. The project is collapsing under the weight of corruption and chicanery engendered by management, both in country and back on the main company board. Sam has to navigate murky waters to get it back on course, not helped by interference from people who want her to fail. When poachers invade the elephant sanctuary next door, her problems multiply. Can Sam protect the elephants and save the project or will she have to choose?

The fourth book in the Sam Harris Series presents Sam with her sternest test yet as she goes to Africa to fix a failing project. The day-to-day problems encountered by Sam in her work are typical of any project manager in the Congo which has been rent apart by warring factions, leaving the local population frightened and rootless. Elephants with pink tusks do exist, but not in the area where the project is based. They are being slaughtered by poachers in Gabon for the Chinese market and will soon be extinct, so I have put the guns in the hands of those responsible for the massacre of these defenceless animals.

The Bonita Protocol - Book 5

An erratic boss. Suspicious results. Stock market shenanigans. Can Sam Harris expose the scam before they silence her? It's 1996. Geologist Sam Harris has been around the block, but she's prone to nostalgia, so she snatches the chance to work in Sierramar, her old stomping ground. But she never expected to be working for a company that is breaking all the rules. When the analysis results from drill samples are suspiciously high, Sam makes a decision that puts her life in peril. Can she blow the lid on the conspiracy before they shut her up for good? The Bonita Protocol sees Sam return to

Sierramar and take a job with a junior exploration company in the heady days before the Bre-X crash. I had fun writing my first megalomaniac female boss for this one. I have worked in a few junior companies with dodgy bosses in the past, and my only comment on the sector is buyer beware…

Digging Deeper - Book 6

A feisty geologist working in the diamond fields of West Africa is kidnapped by rebels. Can she survive the ordeal or will this adventure be her last? It's 1998. Geologist Sam Harris is desperate for money so she takes a job in a tinpot mining company working in war-torn Tamazia. But she never expected to be kidnapped by blood thirsty rebels.

Working in Gemsite was never going to be easy with its culture of misogyny and corruption. Her boss, the notorious Adrian Black is engaged in a game of cat and mouse with the government over taxation. Just when Sam makes a breakthrough, the camp is overrun by rebels and Sam is taken captive. Will anyone bother to rescue her, and will she still be alive if they do?

I worked in Tamazia (pseudonym for a real place) for almost a year in different capacities. The first six months I spent in the field are the basis for this book. I don't recommend working in the field in a country at civil war but, as for many of these crazy jobs, I needed the money.

Concrete Jungle - Book 7 (series end)

Armed with an MBA, Sam Harris is storming the City - But has she swapped one jungle for another?

Forging a new career was never going to be easy, and Sam discovers she has not escaped from the culture of misogyny and corruption that blighted her field career. When her past is revealed, she finally achieves the acceptance she has always craved, but being one of the boys is not the panacea she expected. The death of a new friend presents her with the stark choice of compromising her principals to keep her new position, or exposing the truth behind the façade. Will she finally get what she wants or was it all a mirage?

I did an MBA to improve my career prospects, and much like Sam, found it didn't help much. In the end, it's only your inner belief that counts. What other people say, or think, is their problem. I hope you enjoy this series. I wrote it to rid myself of demons, and it worked.

Box Sets for the Sam Harris Adventure Series are available on Amazon

You can order any of these books in paperback direct from my website. Please go to the PJSKINNER for links or use the QR code below.

Connect with the Author

About the Author

I have been writing in various genres and under various pen names for nearly ten years. In 2020, I moved to a small town on the south coast of England where I spent lockdown during the Covid pandemic. During that time, I published a sci-fi mystery, Mortal Mission under the name of Pip Skinner and realised I had a great idea for a series of Cozy/Cosy Mysteries set at the English seaside. I have always been a massive fan of crime and mystery and I guess it was inevitable I would turn my hand to a mystery series eventually. I planned the Seacastle Mysteries with half an eye on the classic mysteries of Agatha Christie, so they are classic whodunnits.

Before I wrote novels, I spent 30 years working as an exploration geologist, managing remote sites and doing due diligence on projects in over thirty countries. During this time, I worked in many countries in South America and Africa in remote, strange, and often dangerous places where I collected the tall tales and real-life experiences. These inspired the Sam Harris Adventure Series, chronicling the adventures of a female geologist as a pioneer in a hitherto exclusively male world.

Follow me on Amazon to get informed of my new releases. Just put PJ Skinner into the search box on Amazon and then click on the follow button on my author page.

Please subscribe to my Seacastle Mysteries Newsletter for updates and offers by using this QR code

You can also use the QR code below to get to my website for updates and to buy paperbacks direct from me.

You can also follow me on Twitter, Instagram, Tiktok, or on Facebook @pjskinnerauthor

Made in the USA
Coppell, TX
17 June 2024

33606341R00156